TIGER
TIGER

TIGER TIGER

MELVIN BURGESS

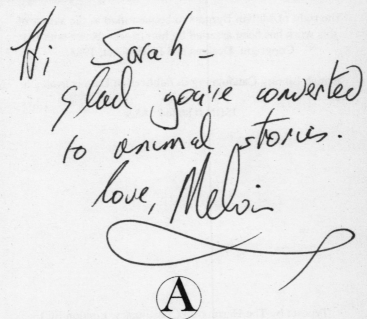

Hi Sarah —
glad you're converted
to animal stories.
love, Melvin

Ⓐ

Andersen Press · London

For Klaus

First published in 1996
by Andersen Press Limited,
20 Vauxhall Bridge Road, London SW1V 2SA

British Library Cataloguing in Publication Data is available

ISBN 0 86264 683 9

Typeset by The Harrington Consultancy, London EC1
Printed and bound in Great Britain by Clays Limited,
Bungay, Suffolk

Contents

Contents

And what shoulders, and what art
Could twist the sinews of thy heart?

William Blake

1

The Tiger Park

The sheep were released at the eastern end of the killing pen. There was a three-mile run all the way from Pikedaw Hill and down to Attermire Scar. People didn't like to see them caught in a corner by the wire, jumping at it in terror, running up and down where there was no way through. They never got that far. The tigers always caught them long before that.

The loudspeakers gave a final warning for the faint-hearted to make their way to the café and visitors' centre before the kill began. A group of over two hundred people waited opposite the gate where the sheep were to be let out. Across the valley a cloud chased, showering rain, and the spectators pulled the hoods of their anoraks close. The rain shone silver in the sunshine. A boy standing apart from the crowd with his father thought ... somewhere there must be a rainbow.

A tall, lean man was speaking to the crowd with a microphone. He was dressed as a Safari Ranger and had sharp blue eyes and a mahogany brown skin. Three years in the Yorkshire Dales hadn't softened the tan of a lifetime under an African sun.

'Ladies and gentlemen, you are about to see something that this part of the world has not witnessed since the Ice Age – big cats going in for the kill. One day these animals are going to have to fend for themselves. No one's going to fetch them butcher's meat in the wild. What you are about to witness is an entirely natural event.'

The spectators peered excitedly to where the sheep stood, milling nervously about in a small pen. Some people stood on tiptoe and looked across the wet slopes, away across Kirkby Fell and along the valley towards Settle. The tigers were nowhere to be seen.

A Range Rover drew up by the sheep pen. A Park Ranger got out and opened the gate. His dog jumped out of the car window, darted through the gate and crouched low in the grass, staring hard at the sheep who huddled together at the far end of the fold. The man followed the dog over the low fence and opened the narrow gate between the sheep fold and the tigers' enclosure.

The dog chivvied at the sheep's heels. One by one the sheep popped out into the open pasture. They looked nervously about and tested the air. There was a dangerous scent on the wind. But these animals had not been hunted for hundreds of years and understood nothing. The grass in the tiger enclosure was long, like a meadow. They quickly dropped their heads and began to graze.

Half a mile off, a group of three tigers appeared from behind a cluster of weathered white rocks and began to stroll down towards the sheep. Their orange and black stripes stood out against the green of the grass like splashes of paint.

'This is the third generation of Siberian tigers that have hunted here,' continued the guide. 'The first generation didn't really know how to go about it. They thought the sheep were playing chase every time they ran off.' The people in the crowd laughed softly. The sheep were so stupid it was almost impossible to feel sorry for them.

Several of the sheep had raised their heads to watch the cats approaching them. Their ears flicked to and fro. As the big cats got nearer the little flock trotted fifty feet up along the valley – not frightened yet, just anxious – moving on to a safer distance from the strange, orange beasts. The tigers continued at the same pace.

'They soon learned there was meat under those woolly coats,' said the guide. He peered through the rain glittering in the pale sunshine. 'It didn't take them long to learn how to hunt and kill prey. These days, the tigers like to spice things up. With a little ambush, perhaps.' He pointed down the slope towards a crooked little tree growing from an outcrop of limestone further down the valley. 'Keep an eye on that hawthorn bush ...'

The crowd peered downhill to where the guide pointed. Half hidden behind the outcrop and trees, two more of the big cats were waiting, crouched low to the ground. The valley would lead the sheep right past them.

The crowd sighed and settled in closer to the fence.

Steve Hattersly, twelve years old, gripped the fence with his hands. He had seen all of this before but it never failed to thrill. The silly sheep had no chance! They didn't know what was going on. And the tigers were perfect – made for killing.

The tigers began to speed up, their bodies low, their faces up to watch the sheep. They began to spread out. Those in the crowd closest to them could hear them calling to each other in low voices, keeping in touch, 'Aoew, aoew.' The sheep began to run just as the rain cloud passed overhead, its shadow quickly overtaking them and disappearing over the hill. Steve's father, standing behind his son, snorted in amusement at the sight of the flock of sheep trotting off to the orange and black death waiting for them a few hundred yards ahead. 'Stupid bloody sheep,' he muttered.

But as he spoke one of the sheep peeled off from the rest of the flock and began to run up the side of the steep valley, away from the ambush. 'That one must be a genius,' said Mr Hattersly. 'It's not telling its mates, though, is it?'

The lone sheep came to a halt. It glanced down at the rest of the flock, as if surprised at what it had done. Its legs twitched.

From the steep valley sides above it came bleating. It sounded as if another sheep was hiding among the rocks up there and was calling to it.

The sheep below jerked its head, to the right, to the left. Then it began to climb laboriously up the side of the valley towards where the call had come from. Steve leaned his head against the cold wire, wet with the rain which had now passed overhead.

'Lila,' he whispered to himself. 'Lila.'

The guide was watching irritably as the lone sheep toiled on up the hillside away from the ambush. He nodded his head down the valley. 'Let's walk down ... see if we can get a better look at the kill,' he said. The visitors began to hurry along the wire. 'Don't run, you'll scare the sheep off,' he called after them.

4

'See the kill, Steve?' asked his father.

Steve looked up. 'Just a minute – I want to see this ...'

The lone sheep was still toiling up the valley side where the turf was thin and the bleached white limestone showed through. Suddenly, as if out of the earth, a tigress arose from the rocks. She made no effort to hide herself. She was only ten metres from the sheep, which stumbled as she came into view but was unable to stop. The tigress bleated again, mockingly. She lay down on her side on a slab of limestone to watch and wait.

Steve held his breath. 'Silly sheep, silly sheep,' he whispered. But it wouldn't have mattered if he'd shouted. The sheep was as good as dead.

'Ridiculous!' His father snorted disgustedly. 'Tigers hunting sheep! They might as well roll cans of cat food down hill.'

Down the valley the three tigers were running fast, their bodies intent, their gaze fixed. Some of the spectators, ignoring the guide, ran along the wire to try and keep up with them. The sheep, truly scared at last, were galloping as fast as they could, their bulging eyes rolling, their clotted fleeces bouncing up and down. They drew level with the hawthorn cluster; the fence creaked as the crowd leaned forward.

The tigers burst from cover roaring. It was shocking – even the crowd by the fence jumped back in fright. The sheep were so taken by surprise that four of them actually fell down in fright. They never got to their feet. Three had their heads almost severed as the great jaws seized their necks. One was swatted and went flying off, bouncing in the long grass with a broken back while its killer, a big male, bounded after a second victim. The remaining sheep scattered and tripped like girls stumbling in the meadow. The tigers ran easily after them. Two of them each seized a sheep by the neck, forced it down to the ground and took the throat in its jaws. There was a long moment as the tigers waited for the sheep to suffocate. The third cat tripped a fleeing sheep with a flick of its paw and took the soft throat in the same deadly grip.

And that was it. The one remaining sheep ran off for a hundred metres and then turned and stood staring at the scene of the kill for a full minute. As the tigers began to feed, the sheep began once more to tear at the long, rich grass.

The guide raised his voice. 'These are natural skills – essential for the tigers if we are ever to reintroduce these magnificent beasts back into the wild.'

There was a spatter of applause. Some people turned away, others watched more closely as the tigers lay by their kills and began to tear the wool away with their teeth. They seemed to be having difficulty getting through the thick fleeces.

'Tigers, unfortunately, can't spit,' pointed out the guide. The spectators giggled.

Steve, waiting further uphill, had watched the kill: it was too dramatic to miss. But now he turned his eyes back to watch what he truly wanted to see – the tigress Lila take her chosen sheep.

The lone sheep had come to a stop on the steep valley side just a few metres away from the waiting tigress, who lay on her rock like an empress on a throne. She watched as the dumb creature stood swaying. Steve had the sensation she was waiting for him to watch her. Lila was a show-off.

The sheep fell suddenly to its knees. Its head hung, as if it were ashamed.

'Drugged,' sneered Steve's dad. 'They've drugged it for her.' The tigress made her way carefully down towards the sheep, which trembled violently as she came right up to stand next to it. She bent her head and neatly closed her jaws around the sheep's soft throat.

'Drugged,' said his dad angrily. 'I expect they all are – it's too easy. Then the drugs get into the tigers and keep 'em tame. They'll never put them back in the wild. It's all a big show, that's all. More profits.' He sighed and spread his hands. 'Well, why not? Good for them, good for us, too, eh, Steve?'

Steve did not answer, he was watching the tigress drag the carcass off out of sight into one of the timber shelters scattered all over the park.

He was waiting. He was certain she knew he was there.

As she was about to disappear into the hide, the eyes of the tigress met those of the boy over the dead sheep. Lila stopped and stared; and her eyes held him and entered him. Just as the sheep had done before him, Steve felt his legs grow weak and his neck turn to jelly. He clung to the wire for support and bowed his head. Were it not for the wire, the tigress could command him to wait, as the sheep had waited, while she padded down to him. And just at that moment, he wouldn't have

7

minded. He was her creature.

The moment passed. Strength returned. Steve pushed himself upright and glanced at his father but the weakness had gone unnoticed. The tigress disappeared into the timber hide.

'Lila,' whispered Steve. Lila was magic.

He always sought her out when he went to the Tiger Park, which he did almost every week. She did this to him from time to time. It was a sort of game. Lila liked to tease him.

'Her name?' said a voice behind him.

Steve jumped. The voice was that of an elderly man but it seemed to be coming from right behind his neck. He spun round. Behind him was a tiny man, no bigger than he was. A Chinese, he was immaculately dressed in a black suit with an open shirt. His black eyes did not meet Steve's. The skin on his face was stretched tight over his face, and networked with hundreds of tiny, fine lines. He looked very, very old and ill, but his hair was pitch black and his eyes were full of curiosity and strength.

He bowed slightly and smiled politely. 'Excuse me. Lila – is that her name?' Steve just stared. He had never seen anyone like him before. The man cocked his head, expecting – commanding – an answer.

'Yes, Lila,' Steve replied. 'She's still quite young, she's only just reached maturity. She should be taking her first mate soon.' Steve knew everything about all the tigers in the Park.

The Chinese man smiled broadly. 'Thank you,' he said politely. 'Thank you, thank you.' He took three or four steps away and turned for a last look at the hide where the tigress was devouring her kill.

By seven the last of the visitors had driven off. One or two walkers made their way past the perimeter fence as the light faded, trying to catch a free glimpse of the tigers. Nicky Abbot, the Park guide, and his wife Sheila, who managed the restaurant and café in the Tiger Park, were chatting in the lobby outside the souvenir shop as Mike Craven, the Park Director, walked past with his arms full of folders.

'Busy tonight?' Nicky called.

Mike pulled a face. 'Creditors,' he growled. The Tiger Park was an expensive business. Tonight, as every night, there would be five guards on alert in case anything went wrong. Plus video cameras, electric fences, double lock gates. There were many visitors to the Park, but not enough. They were losing money fast.

'Trying to get another stay of execution,' he complained.

'Will it really come to that?' Nicky wanted to know.

'Basically they want me to go on with it. Well – things'll work out – tonight, anyway. 'Night!'

'Goodnight. And good luck!'

Mike left the building, loaded up his Range Rover and drove off. Sheila locked the door to the restaurant.

'Ready?'

'Okay.'

'You drive, would you? I have a few points I need to work out...'

Nicky nodded briefly. His wife had the same dry

brown skin and pale blue eyes. They had lived and worked in the game parks of East Africa for over ten years, before they had returned to England to work at Malham for Mike. They walked together across the tarmac in front of the visitors' centre to the car, and drove off. They had to drive to Manchester for an important meeting.

Inside the building, the security guards got out cards, books, cigarettes, Thermos flasks. They settled down for what would be another long boring night.

When all trace of the sun had gone and the people who covered these hills like lice were all safely tucked away at home, Lila emerged from the timber frame hut where she slept and sniffed the night. She could smell everything – sheep, grass, small mammals, tigers. She could smell the weather – the wind, the clouds in the sky. Even the moonlight gave the world under its silver light a cool, fresh scent.

To Lila, who had spent the first few months of her life in a small paddock at Whipsnade Zoo with her mother, the three hundred square miles of Dales upland that made up Malham Tiger Park was no more than a paddock. The animals here were all Siberians, the biggest of all tigers. Back in the thin forests where they had originated, this whole park would not provide a territory for even one of them. Here, there lived over twenty. The males had to be let out in ones and twos, taking turns to be kept in the central holding block, or there would have been fights. The females, like Lila, were allowed to range free.

The hunting, too, was ridiculous; even the native Siberian reindeer were no match for the tiger, let alone the fat, inbred sheep and little roe and munkjak deer that the park released. To most of the tigers, all of whom had been captive bred, the park represented the richest environment they had ever known. Only Lila had the imagination to guess, as she sniffed at the air and twitched her ears, that this was more truly a desert than the snowy, frozen lands she was born for.

Sheep, dogs and men, that's all it was. A few rodents. The Dales were a desert indeed. Stripped long ago of trees and wildlife, the beautiful open hills and empty rugged views held only a fraction of the variety they had once known. There were rabbits and hares. Lila and the others often came out at night to hunt the rabbits who crept through the wire after the long, rich grass, untrimmed by sheep. They were at least wild – some sport for the bored cats.

But it was not rabbits Lila sought tonight.

However poor this land might be in the scents of plants and animals, it was rich in one respect – the scents and sounds of her own kind. Tigers make a great variety of noises beyond the familiar growls, snarls and roars. With her keen ears, Lila could pick out what half the colony were doing. Four miles away, two adolescent males, Timba and Shere Khan, were tracking for rabbits in the dark. They called to each other in the darkness with soft, penetrating cries – ahoo, ahoo – pinpointing each other's position. Further along the perimeter fence, Tiny, the biggest of them all, grunted to himself as he dug a vast hole in the ground in his timeless attempt to find a way out of the park. He never would; the wire was set in reinforced concrete a metre deep, in the limestone base. Which was just as well. Tiny weighed nearly eight hundred pounds and could have taken the roof off a car with a blow of his paw.

Tiny lifted his head and sniffed the air. He climbed out of his hole and woofed. He too could smell something. Tonight for the first time, Lila was in season.

All the tigers had their own territories, overlapping each other. In order to release more than one big male each night, the park was divided into three by tall fences. These fences had doors built into them, small enough for the females to creep through, but not the big males. Lila was within Tiny's area now. He called to her again, but Lila kept her silence and crept off to get downwind of him and away from his section. Tiny kept track of her with his nose, pacing up and down the wire of his territory. Shortly he began roaring his rage and frustration.

Lila wandered on north through the lush grass. She paused every now and then to sniff at scent markings or to listen – to munkjak deer running along by the fence, to mice and rats and voles hiding in the grass roots. Other tigers were calling, but Lila stayed quiet. She did not need to call. Her communication tonight was with her scent. Not until she found the spray markings of Sirrah, a male about two years older than her, did she utter a short, strange call in a human-like voice ...

'Tok! Tok!'

There was a short pause before Sirrah answered in the same way. Lila stood, the tip of her tail waving slightly, and stared deeply into the darkness where the noise had come from. She turned round excitedly and sprayed urine on the remains of a drystone wall where he had marked earlier that night. He called again – much closer now. Lila barked back excitedly, but ran off into the night. If he wanted her, he would have to find her ...

Sirrah was not the biggest, or oldest, or the most powerful of the Park tigers, although he was certainly a magnificent beast. But as with people, so with tigers ... for some reason he was the one who had taken her fancy. Lila being Lila, she would be the one to choose her mate.

Out of the darkness Sirrah emerged where she had stood. He sniffed the wall where Lila had sprayed, then squirted urine to make his mark. In the distance, Lila called; another male answered her: Tiny. Sirrah looked positively alarmed. He was scared of Tiny. He did not really understand that the big tiger was unable to come to this part of the park. But that made no difference. Sirrah was infatuated. He began to run swiftly after the object of his desire. He did not have to go far or chase her for long.

The same evening, eighty miles away in a hotel room in Manchester, four people met to discuss a very profitable crime. One of them was the same guide who had taken the sightseers round the Tiger Park earlier that same day – Nicky Abbot. Another, his wife, Sheila. A third was

Lee Yung, the Hong Kong businessman who had spoken to Steve earlier that day. He sat perched in a large, comfortable-looking armchair, but it was so much too big for him he made it look uncomfortable, like a strange, ancient boy pretending to be grown up. The last, a young man, was bending down to a cabinet in a corner of the room. He served drinks to the other three, then bowed and backed off to stand in one corner, as if he were an ornament or a piece of furniture rather than a living person.

'All of them,' said Mr Lee quietly when the man had moved away.

The guide, Nicky Abbot, pulled a face and scratched his chin. 'It'd have to be done in one night ...' he began.

'That is why you must get them all,' observed Mr Lee. 'There will be only one chance.'

'Getting out four or five, that's one thing. Slaughtering the whole park ...'

'One man to drive a lorry,' said Sheila crisply. 'Five men to carry one tiger easily, Nicky?' Her husband nodded and hid his nose in his drink, thoroughly alarmed at the way the talk was going. He wanted to make a bit of money. But this ...

'Say, four teams of five working together. Lookouts, driver. Twenty-five people at the minimum. The minimum. People willing to do this sort of thing want plenty of money.'

'I will supply all the men you want.'

She pulled a face. She didn't like that. But there was sense in it. They hadn't the contacts here that they used to have in Africa. 'The risk ...' she complained. 'The more people involved the more risk ...'

'It's all right for you, you'll be out of the country,' blurted Nicky to the businessman. 'We'll have to sit here and sweat it out.'

Mr Lee smiled vaguely at Nicky, as if in sympathy. How unfortunate that the man was nervous. He was greedy as well, of course, but if you were going to be greedy you'd better be hard as well. Like the wife. It was her he addressed.

'My clients are rich men, very desperate to get this medicine,' he observed. 'Tigers, you know, are at a premium. I can charge what I like.' He smiled joyfully. 'So can you.' He nodded enthusiastically to make sure she understood this point.

Sheila Abbot raised an eyebrow. 'Not a very business-like remark,' she said, with a wry smile.

'It's necessary to pay well for quality goods. These goods will not be available for much longer. Quite possibly you are the last supplier in the world.' He smiled again. 'If I may offer a bit of advice, from one businessman to another – you should be careful not to undercharge.'

Sheila nodded curtly.

'And what will you do,' Nicky wanted to know, 'when the supply runs out?'

Mr Lee cocked his head curiously. 'Change my business, Mr Abbot,' he explained patiently.

Nicky shook his head irritably. 'What about conserving your business instead?'

Mr Lee smiled sadly. The man was an idiot. 'I admire the tigers too, Mr Abbot,' he explained. 'They are the most magnificent creatures. That's why they are such good medicine. But what I do for money, what you do for money, makes no difference to the tigers. They are passing out of this world. Already they're just ghosts, living in this strange land, hunting sheep.' He laughed down his nose at the thought. 'I shall be sorry to see them go, but their time is over. They are anachronisms. If not me, you. If not you, someone else – or the rain in this country. Or they will choke on the wool. Or the land will swallow them. So.' He spread his hands in resignation. 'As the Americans say, I'm in it for the ride. Why not?'

Later, on the drive home to Grassington, Nicky voiced his doubts.

'*All* of them,' he complained. 'I'm doing myself out of a job, apart from anything.'

Sheila snorted her derision. 'You won't need a job, Nicky.'

'I like my job.'

'Don't you miss Africa? We could move back. We could buy the place with the money I'm going to charge.'

'What are you going to charge?'

Sheila said, 'Millions.'

'Joking aside ...'

'I mean it. Millions. A couple of them, I'd say.'

Sheila watched her husband's face as he took this in. His face flared up in the light from an oncoming lorry. His lips moved. He was mouthing – two million ...

'What about the risk?' he asked. He bit his lip and

16

glanced anxiously at her. 'All of them! It's too dangerous.'

'What danger?' she wanted to know. 'Anaesthetic darts, the right poison, they won't even squeak. Justin's with us; the rest of the guards can be dealt with easily enough. We can have all the men we want. I foresee no difficulties.'

He pulled a face.

'You're not getting scruples are you?' she asked. 'You never worried about poaching in Africa.'

'That was different.'

'Oh? Why?'

'The Tiger Park is an important project ...'

'Oh, don't give me that,' she snapped. 'Like the man said, these beasts are on the way out. No one's ever going to introduce them back into the wild, you know that. Where would they do it? All the reserves are completely overrun. They stand as much chance surviving in the wild in the streets of Manchester as they would in Siberia. You've told me that often enough yourself.'

He couldn't deny it.

'All those years of breaking the law and risking our necks in Africa and nothing to show for it. Now we get a chance to really make money and you get squeamish ...'

'Tell you the truth, I like the job and I like the tigers, too. I've got to know them. That's the difference.'

'Pet cats,' she sneered. 'I'll buy you a Persian with the money, if you like them that much. Someone else will get there if we don't do it, you must know that. That sort of money. Those cats might as well be dead now.'

He nodded glumly.

'You'll do it then?'

Nicky paused, but only for effect. He nodded. Sheila put her hand on her husband's shoulder and patted him.

'But all of them,' he complained. 'What if we missed four or five out? Things go wrong, after all.'

She gazed across at him. 'Any favourites?'

Nicky smiled without amusement. 'Yes, but you won't like it.'

'Don't tell me. Lila.' She turned away and half laughed, as if in despair.

'That cat has more personality than any animal I've ever seen – more than most people,' he insisted. 'Have you seen what she can do with the sheep? She doesn't *need* to hunt, that tiger.'

'You remember what Lee said, don't you?'

He remembered. Before they went, the Hong Kong businessman had held up his hand to make an important point.

'Please remember. One of these cats is for me. The young tigress – Lila. That one is special. A Spirit Tiger. Very special. Very rare. Once in a hundred generations. You see, I am an old man. Very sick man. Did you know?' He glanced at Nicky and his wife, who shook their heads.

'Oh, yes. Cancer,' said Mr Lee. He nodded brightly, as if he was talking about a nice day tomorrow. Nicky and Sheila glanced at each other. Of course they had noticed how shrivelled and thin the old man was, and they had wondered what the matter was. Even the bones of his nose stood out sharply under his pale, thin skin.

'I have been told I have maybe a year to live, but ... I have too much to live for to be ready to die. The bones and organs of the tiger have special properties, as you know. Those of the Spirit Tiger are most remarkable. Very good indeed. Super special. Long life. You understand me? That one I want at all costs. Like my clients I am rich and desperate. I will pay well. Lila is for me.'

Back in the car Nicky snorted his contempt. 'Spirit Tiger. Load of hocus pocus.'

'Money is magic,' observed Sheila. She opened her handbag and fished around inside for a mint to suck. 'Want one?' She held out a packet of Polos. Nicky shook his head. Sheila popped one in her mouth and sucked. She clipped her bag shut and said crisply, 'It may be possible to save one or two of the others. But I'm afraid Lila has to die.'

2

Massacre

On the night, as it turned out, everything was perfect. Sheila had it all organised to the last second – you had to hand it to her. And they had luck; even the weather was on their side. The night was perfect, pitch black.

Inside the block everyone was talking in whispers, including the Chinese gangsters Mr Lee had provided. But Sheila came in with her clipboard to run over the final details and didn't even bother to lower her voice. When she saw Nicky looking alarmed she shrugged and smiled. 'No one's going to hear us now,' she observed, nodding towards the observation room where the night guards lay, trussed and drugged. A hypodermic in the arm was all it took to put them away for the night. Only Justin was still awake, manning the cameras and the telephone. And he was on their side.

After that everyone talked normally. Nicky, who had taken the trouble to wear a balaclava back to front with holes for his eyes, felt overdressed. It was as if they were organising the final stages of a village fête.

Nicky distributed the rifles that would fire the lethal darts while Sheila ran through the details and the timing with the men yet again. There were four teams of six men. The leading man from each team would go along the neat rows of cages and fire through the bars. The killing would be silent. The tigers' drinking water had been drugged. They wouldn't even know they were dying.

Death would take approximately two minutes. At this point the remaining members of the team could enter, and drag or carry the carcasses out to be loaded into the waiting lorry. The whole thing – over twenty deaths – should be completed in half an hour.

Normally the tigers would have slept out in the enclosure but there had been a veterinary examination that night, which of course was why Sheila had picked it. The central block was an hexagonal building. Each side of the hexagon held five cages. Four sides were full tonight; two more had three beasts. The twenty-six tigers who lived in the colony represented over a quarter of the world's total population of Siberian tigers.

At a nod from Sheila, the four teams set off.

Nicky Abbot led his team of five to the cages he had responsibility for. First was Tiny, the biggest male, who entertained the crowd by taking full grown bullocks. Then there was dear old Sarah, who had founded the colony, almost: more than half the tigers there had some of her blood in them. Then a male called Ruddy, named after Rudyard Kipling. Then Lila, the so-called Spirit Tiger. It was several months since Mr Lee had made that first visit to the Tiger Park. These things took time to organise. Now, Lila had two cubs, her first young. She was a magnificent tiger, almost as big as some of the males, despite her youth. Finally there was Donna Bella, Lila's mother, still in her prime.

Nicky was in a hurry, although he knew the half-hour allowed was just for guidance. Actually, they had all night. But he'd be glad when this night's work was over. On the one hand it was all so simple, he felt that he was already rich. On the other – who knew what could happen? He was superstitious about tigers. And anyway, the night was not without danger. He didn't like to be surrounded by all these Chinese gangsters. Triad members. The Chinese mafia were notorious for their cruelty, and Nicky was uncomfortably aware that now they were here with everything set up, he and Sheila were suddenly unnecessary.

One of the Chinese shone a torch into the first cage. Tiny lay sleeping on his side, dead to the world. Normally the torch beam would have been enough to wake the big male, but tonight he slept on, peaceful as a lamb. If you looked closely you could see from his shallow, shuddering breaths that he was not asleep, but unconscious from the drugged drinking water.

Nicky took aim, resting the gun on his forearm. He pulled the trigger. There was a noise like a suppressed sneeze and the dart appeared as if by magic on Tiny's shoulder. Tiny lifted his head. Briefly his eyes met those of his killers. His lips began to curl and he made the beginnings of a snarl. He plucked at the dart in his shoulder with his teeth. Then his head fell back. His heart had already stopped.

Sarah didn't even stir. Poor old girl, thought Nicky. The tranquilliser in her water had probably been enough to top her off. In the third cage Ruddy was awake, as if he knew something was afoot. He was trying to walk away when they came across him, but his hind legs kept giving way underneath him. He turned to watch as Nicky fired the dart.

Nicky was irritated. What was the beast doing

awake? Well, even Sheila couldn't be sure the tigers would drink all the water they needed to put them out. Even so, he had to admit that with tranquilliser in the water, poison darts, a gun in his belt and bars between him and the tigers it was a safe enough business. But you couldn't call it sport.

The fourth cage: Lila. The Spirit Tiger, Mr Lee had called her. All a load of old monkey. But you could see his point. There was something about her all right.

By this time Nicky was into the rhythm – shoot, load a new dart, step to the next cage, aim, fire. He didn't even want to think about this one. He'd have saved her if he could. Sheila had tried to get a couple of the others off the hook, but the presence of the Chinese made saving any of them impossible, as Sheila must have known right from the start.

There she lay, in deep sleep, the cubs curled up against her side like soft toys. He could see the sides of the three animals fitfully rising and falling, rising and falling, as if each breath was their last. Full of dope, all three.

Nicky raised the rifle and fired. He hit Lila on the shoulder; he saw clearly how the skin around the wound shuddered slightly, how her ears twitched. But the tigress lay still. Now the cubs. His men carried spare rifles so he could deal with all three quickly. He was aware of a murmur of surprise from his men as he took the first rifle and fired it into one of the cubs. Then he reached out for the next rifle, but the man who held it was backing off.

'Boss?' said the man. He sounded alarmed

'What is it?' Nicky asked irritably.

The man pointed into the cage. Nicky followed his finger, but it was just an empty corner of the cage. 'The gun, man!' he demanded. But one of the Chinese leaned forward and snatched the gun off the first man. There was a sudden babble of talk. Then the man rapidly fired the rifle, not at the two tiger cubs, but at the empty corner of the cage.

The balaclava suddenly began to itch with sweat. 'What's going on, what's your game?' demanded Nicky angrily. For a second he was convinced it was a trick. They would kill him, next.

'You missed the bloody tigers. Look!' insisted the Chinese in a Manchester accent. He pointed again; again, the empty corner of the cage, the concrete floor, straw on which nothing lay.

What was going on? Nicky could see as clear as day the three tigers, two of them with the darts sticking out of them, their sides now still. Only the last cub needed fixing. He stared transfixed as it rubbed its face into its mother's coat, stretched, mewed, and then settled back down to innocent sleep.

Nicky stared from the tigers to the men. He felt sick; it was all going beyond him for no reason at all ...

There was a sudden burst of Chinese from one of the men. He was clearly the leader – the real leader, Nicky realised. The other men began to back off while this man gesticulated and shouted at them in rapid Chinese. Nicky could understand none of it but one phrase in English ...

'Spirit Tiger,' one of them was saying. 'Spirit Tiger ...' The shouting man had taken a handgun out of his jacket.

This was getting out of hand ...

'Look ...' Nicky wanted urgently to show the men that it was all right, that everything was going according to plan – to take the situation back in hand. He took the electronic key to the cages out of his pocket. 'The tiger is already dead,' he promised them with a smile. He inserted the key in the lock and pushed.

As the door swung open, the image of Lila lying on her side vanished. She appeared instead in the empty corner of the cage running fast towards him, her eyes were fixed on him; she was hunting. The five men screamed and ran. Nicky lost a second in amazement, then fumbled at the door to get it shut. But Lila was on him. She shoved him away from the door with one paw, hooked the other round the bars and drew the door open towards her. Nicky got to his knees; she swatted him, knocking him flying, and ran swiftly down the corridor to the side door that led out into the enclosure. One of the Chinese shot at her but missed. The door was locked; she flung herself at it with her full weight and went straight through, taking door, door frame and a hundredweight of rubble with her. They heard her steps outside. Then, stillness. The cold night wind blew in on them. It had all taken about ten seconds.

The Chinese had turned at the opposite end of the corridor and stood in a group. One of them was holding a gun in a trembling hand. There was a low rumble from the last cage, like some tired huge old man. Donna was waking up.

Nicky got to his feet. He felt sick from the violent bruising he had just taken, as well as from the shock of realising that he could no longer trust his senses. A flood of excited Chinese chatter came down the corridor at him, probably abuse.

'Fetch Sheila, tell her what's happened. I'm going after her,' he yelled. He ran down towards the crushed door. He paused before he went out. The five Chinese stood, watching him curiously. Nicky looked sternly at them. He was impressing them. Triad they might be, but none of them cared to go out after the tigress. He scrambled over the door and outside.

Nicky ran three steps and stopped. It was like a wall of darkness out there. It was raining. Always the filthy rain here! Nicky longed for the hot skies and earth of Africa. It was so dark – too dark for him. But not for Lila.

Nicky held his gun up by his ear, ready to bring his arm out and fire. He stood very still, listening, but his breath rasped and his heart pounded violently inside him. All he could hear was a tawny owl calling, miles off over the park.

He was wasting his time. The park was enormous. Lila would be miles away by now.

Nicky pulled the balaclava up over his head and let the cool air brush over him. He wiped his mouth on the back of his hand. What on earth had happened? He'd seen her so clearly in the cage! He'd seen everything – the cubs, their sides rising up and down as they breathed – even the way Lila's ears twitched as the dart pierced her skin.

The tiger had made him see her where she never was.

There was a slight noise to the right and he turned,

lifting the gun. The attack, of course, came from the left.

'Where?' Sheila burst on the five men without warning. She saw them jump. They were full of nerves, standing in a group by the door. One of them waved a gun at the broken door at the other end of the corridor.

'What are you doing with a bloody gun, you heard my orders, only Nicky should have a gun.'

The man smiled tightly. 'There's a tiger loose,' he said. Sheila decided to ignore the break in discipline.

'And Nicky?'

'He went after it ...'

'God!' What on earth for, the bloody tiger would be miles away by now ....

She took two steps down the corridor and then turned to the men. 'Get on with it!' she snapped.

The men looked at each other. One of them glared angrily. He obviously didn't like to take orders from a woman. Sheila had no time for that. 'You ...' She pointed to one of the men, who looked the most inclined to be ordered about. 'You keep watch in case she comes back. The rest, load those tigers on. Do you want paying or not? I don't think Mr Lee will be very happy ...' she added when they lingered.

Sheila ran forward and grabbed hold of Tiny's corpse, which had been dragged half out of his cage. Slowly the men came forward to help her.

It weighed a ton, a dead weight. Terrible when you remembered how he had soared and leapt over the grass when he was alive. Sheila was itching to get off and find Nicky, to see if he was safe and find out what was going on, but she was scared the men would abandon their task if she left them. They had got the carcass out of the cage and a few metres across the floor when there was a single gunshot from outside.

'Get him loaded – I'll go and see,' she shouted over her shoulder, off down the corridor. With any luck, Nicky would have killed the wretched beast.

She stuck her head outside. It was raining hard now; she could feel it soaking quickly into her hair.

'Nicky? Nicky, where are you? What's going on?'

There was no answer, only the steady hiss of the rainfall. Sheila drew her pistol and stepped cautiously out. She had got about ten steps from the door when she tripped over something. She pushed herself up and her hand slipped on wet, still flesh. She fumbled at her belt for a torch and clicked it on.

It was Nicky.

She stared at the familiar face. He looked surprised. In one temple was a neat, round bullet hole.

The significance of this sank slowly in as she stared. A bullet hole. A gun fired. Another person ...

She looked up, glanced this way, that way. Were they watching her, aiming at her? The rain seemed to sizzle as she leapt to her feet and ran for the door in terror for her life. As she tripped over the wet rubble at the doorway someone shouted, 'The tigers are loose – they're out!'

Roaring broke out from several parts of the building and outside in the compound as Sheila ran up the corridor. There were men yelling in fright. Passing the first cage she saw that the door was now open and the tigress, Donna, was staggering towards her. Outside the door, bright against the grey tiles, were a set of bare human footprints in bright red blood.

Sheila didn't pause, she would have run faster if she could, straight on past the men who stood in a group around the body of Tiny.

'Get out! Get out of here! There's someone else here – get out ...'

The men dropped Tiny and ran for the truck. For God's sake, whoever it was could be on the telephone right now! Then there was a scream, piercing and shocking, like a girl, amid the snarls of a tiger. It came from one of the other wings. Sheila was heading for the van fast but as she passed the central block she saw a tiger, bending over something that lay on the floor. The thing was a man. He writhed, then lay still. The tiger looked up: it was Lila. Her muzzle red. Men were pouring from all three wings now and the tiger leapt forward, close on their heels.

Sheila shoved the big swing door open and jumped for the van. She got inside and fumbled at the key. As she turned it over she glanced though the glass door inside the building. The gangmen were running to and fro like mice, Lila was among them, chivvying them, swatting at them, jumping on them and savaging them with a twist of her powerful neck. The Triad members were completely at her mercy. She could see one or two waving guns in the air, but they did not fire for fear of hitting a friend in the mêlée.

Roaring was coming from all around now. Whoever it was must have opened a number of cages. There was total panic. Everyone tried to dive into the van at the same time. Sheila let out the clutch, but the van stalled. Cursing she got it going again, but the same thing happened. She felt she was cursed. Men were streaming out of the hexagon, climbing onto the van, hanging from the doors.

'Get out the way!' screamed Sheila. The van stalled again. Then, Lila came. She leaned up on her hind legs to push the door open, then leapt forward. She was right there with them. She ran in a couple of bounds to the van, jumped up on her hind legs and began to snatch at men hanging from the doors of the van. She shook them in her teeth like rats and flung them to the ground behind her where they squirmed in the rain. Two more tigers, still thick with dope, hung back, snarling. One, Sirrah, Lila's mate, was making little runs at the men and then dashing back, as if plucking up his courage to attack. But he was so doped that his legs kept collapsing under him.

There was a shot. Sirrah fell on his side. Lila jumped backwards off the van. One of the men, the gun still in his hand, shoved Sheila out of the way and got the van going – she had forgotten the handbrake, of all the stupid things. The van shot forward. The man tossed his gun to another who fired rapidly back at the tigers as they drove off. Others were chasing the van, screaming not to be left behind. But no one cared anything for anybody now, except to get away.

All the way down the road into Malham and beyond to Skipton, Sheila was expecting the police, the wail of the siren, the sudden glitter of blue lights. But they never came.

As the van roared jerkily off down the road there was a cry of despair from behind her and the sound of feet running. Lila turned and made to run after three men who had been left behind but through the crystal vision of her rage came a strange noise from Sirrah. Her mate had been hit. She turned and ran to see him.

The tigress had managed to save three – Sirrah, Will, another young male, and Donna, her mother. The others – twenty-two of the rarest animals in the world – all lay dead. Some were in the van now bumping its way towards Malham but most were scattered about the compound like slaughtered chickens, in the corridors where they had been dragged or the cages that had become execution cells.

Lila had no idea what had happened or why – only that the people at the park had turned on her and hers. Friends had become enemies. She would not let it happen again. She had to get herself and the three remaining tigers away and to safety.

Tigers are solitary animals much of the time. Confused, frightened, and in Sirrah's case badly wounded, the other tigers' first instinct was to run off alone. Lila was the most junior among them, but they were drugged and deeply confused whilst she was clear headed. She was able to half lead them, half chase them up the hills away from the park and higher into the Dales, to try and find a hiding place.

It was slow going, for tigers. They covered only ten miles in three hours, what with staggering, sitting down and forgetting, and going off in the wrong direction.

Lila was beside herself with frustration. But by this time the drugs were beginning to wear off and Donna and Will were picking up speed. But Sirrah was actually slowing down. A bullet was lodged in the barrel of his chest and now the pain and loss of blood were beginning to tell on him.

Lila turned back and chased him, chivvied him, rubbed herself against him, but he was getting impatient with her. The other tigers were spreading out and soon they would be separated.

At last Sirrah sat down. He coughed; a flood of blood, black in the night, appeared suddenly on his white ruff. He lay down on his side, panting heavily.

Lila had to hide him.

Donna and Will were sitting some way off, watching incuriously. Donna came over to investigate; Will paced impatiently by the rocks. He wanted to be off. What business of his was it that Sirrah was ill? Lila called to him, 'Ahoo, ahoo.' He ignored her. She called again – but with a snarl of impatience he bounded off, paused for a second against the sky on a boulder, and was suddenly gone.

There was nothing Lila could do. And in fact, it was probably right to do nothing. Sirrah was weak, maybe dying. He would only burden them. But he was Lila's first mate and she could not leave him.

Now Donna began to walk off after Will. Desperately, Lila called after her. Donna turned to watch. In the darkness, Will called. Donna turned, listened, and without looking back ran off to find him, leaving her daughter alone with the wounded male.

Lila had to hide Sirrah and then go after the others and make sure they were safely hidden before the dawn, and the men, came back.

She didn't have to look far for the hiding place. Nearby was one of the caves cut into the soft limestone thousands of years ago by the melting ice cap. The small entrance, where a stream fell underground, was only a hundred or so yards off. It led to a network of channels, underground caves, rivers and lakes that spread for miles under the Dales. Under the earth it was dark and cool, an ideal hospital for a tiger.

Lila found her way past a number of passages until she found one suitable, with water running through for the wounded male to drink, and space for him to lie in the dry. Also, the opening was small. Sirrah himself was only just able to squeeze through. Lila would be able to lock him in.

Once inside, he lay on his side, his breath coming in small gasps. Lila sat by him and licked his head, his muzzle, the place on his side where the blood welled. But she could not reach the bullet deep inside him. She transformed herself in the way that was unique to her and tried to probe inside the wound, but Sirrah lashed out at her. If he hit her while she was like that he would kill her.

Now she had done all she could for Sirrah. It was time to try and find the other two. Before she went, Lila piled stones up over the entrance and washed it with water to try and hide her scent. She was transformed again as she emerged from underground and raced out under the sky as herself.

A small high crescent moon had risen and weaved in and out of the clouds as Lila ran swiftly, criss-crossing the even grass till she found the place where Donna and Will had left her. Then she began to track.

The two tigers for some reason had doubled back and begun to return down towards Malham, much to Lila's distress. Whether they had become confused or, despite everything, still did not understand how dangerous man was, she did not know. Some miles above Malham, she found their tracks crossing those of two men and her heart leapt. Had they, like her, felt the urge for revenge? No tiger would normally feel such a desire ...

Soon there was no doubt that the two cats were following the men, but only for a short way. They may have been hoping to be fed. Where the human and tiger tracks separated, Lila paused, undecided. The tigers had headed down to the village. The two men were heading towards the cove. She ought to go after her own kind. But ...

In the end, Lila followed the men. Her blood was up. Why should her kind die and these creatures live? Men did not move fast. She could catch up with the tigers afterwards. The business did not take long. She found them walking the low hills above Malham Cove. People sleeping in a campsite twenty metres from the kill heard nothing.

The delay cost her dear. By the time she found Will and Donna, the sky was already light. She was descending down into the village of Malham when she saw them in a pasture by the roadside, chasing sheep in a field close to Malham. At the same moment as Lila caught her first glimpse of them, she heard the noise of an engine. A Land-Rover was heading down the road into the village. The road would take it right past the field. The driver would see everything.

It was so wretched ... She could not tell them anything or make them understand. Will and Donna had no idea what the Land-Rover meant. But then, neither did Lila. It would have been better for the tigers if the driver, a farmer beginning his long day's work on the hillsides, had spotted them after all. He would have reported it and they could have been caught away from the village where there would have been no fear for human life. Instead, in her efforts to lure them away from the road, Lila drove Donna and Will directly towards Malham village.

As she greeted them she managed to lead them into the next field and into a great abandoned stone barn. The farmer passed by none the wiser that there were three tigers nearby. The three cats rubbed heads and sniffed one another. Will sprayed around the stone walls, marking new territory. Later that day the cattle would refuse to enter. On the other side of the barn was a single narrow field before Malham.

Will was full of himself, delighted at being out on his own with two females. Lila could do nothing to lead him. He thought her approaches were some form of play and frolicked about among the stones, bounding out of an empty doorway and across the rutted mud where the cows crossed in winter to get to the fodder stored in the old barn. Lila ran the other way but he ignored her. He jumped up onto the wall before the village, silhouetted perfectly against the white sky for all to see for miles around, and stared curiously at the houses. His ears twitched at the sound of an engine starting up in the next road, at the sound of the milkman rattling bottles, the postmistress two hundred yards away rolling up the shutters and taking in the morning papers.

Lila ran fast towards him, prepared to drag him backwards by his tail and start a fight if she had to, although Will weighed a hundred pounds more than she did and could probably kill her. Another car started up nearby; they heard human voices. Will paused, uncertain. The events of the night, dulled by the drugs, had been all but forgotten. Now they came back. His lips drew back in a half snarl. He dropped over the wall and into the village. Lila, running full pelt after him, cleared the six-foot wall in a single bound, landing in the middle of a small flagged yard just as the milkman drove round the corner. She and Will sank low on their bellies and slid into some rosebushes and ornamental shrubs growing in a bed right up against the walls. They were in the yard of a converted barn.

The milkman drew up on the road before the house, jumped out of his van and gathered a delivery of milk bottles from his van into his crate. He walked up to the front door not three metres – a single jump – away from the two tigers watching his back intently from among the shrubs. Their stripes, curiously, provided a perfect camouflage among the stems and dappled leaves of the roses.

Will crouched low, his eyes fixed intently on the man.

36

He began to knead the soil with his front paws. All the circumstances were right for an attack. The man was bending low, busy with his bottles. His back was to the tiger. He was between the tiger and the way out of the yard. And Will was confused, angry and afraid.

The milkman clattered bottles, scooping up the empties into his crate. Will stared like a demon at his back, padding with his front paws; he was preparing to spring. But it was at this moment that Donna appeared on the wall above. The male tiger stopped his gathering spring to glance up at her. For a long three or four seconds, Donna, poised on the coping stones atop the wall, stared at the milkman. Then, as he straightened up from the doorstep, she twisted round and dropped sideways, landing neatly in between the rosebushes and the wall. She sank at once to her belly and settled, licking her face. She performed her initial leap onto the wall and her drop from it with such perfection that the milkman, the length of two men distant from her, never heard her land. But as she fell she brushed slightly against the bushes. The milkman heard the leaves stir and turned to stare at the place. In doing so he saved his life.

At the sight of the man standing upright and of his face, Will lay flat once more. The milkman stared for a few seconds. Parts of all three cats showed through the stems and leaves, but their stripes, so vivid on the grass, had made them invisible. Completely ignorant of his near-death encounter, the man turned and walked back to his van, got in and drove off.

The three tigers left their hiding place amongst the roses and walked into the yard, looking astonishingly exotic against the long views, weathered stones and bare walls of the Dalesland village. With their heads raised, they sniffed at the strange air lifting in the village.

Lila was desperately searching for something familiar. So many scents – of car tyres, of cows, of shoes and flowers and stone, of cigarette smoke and diesel, of strange flowers and leaves, of tarmac, bread and butter, bacon cooking. And so many people passed this way! So much of it was strange, so much of it was unhelpful. But among the scents of the many people was one she knew, the only familiar thing in this sea of trouble.

It was the scent of someone she had thought of as a friend. Lila did not like it. She had seen how treacherous human beings were, but ... What could she do but believe, against all experience, that this friend would stay a friend? She had to dare to hope.

Lila emerged from the yard and ran along the road until she came to a long low building. It was desperately urgent – cars were about, voices were on the streets. It was full daylight. They could be discovered any minute. There was a place to hide in this building where a friend lived. The door was locked, but Lila knew how to deal with that. She opened it, slipped in and called,

'Ahoo ... ahoo!'

Will and Donna heard and followed her in. Lila had found their hiding place for the day.

It was a stupid place, really, everything was wrong with it. It was close to men, right in the middle of the village. She had not even had a chance to conceal their tracks. All that could be said for it was, it had a single ray of hope.

Will and Donna, tired after the night's run, fell asleep quickly. They had no idea of the danger they were in. What had a tiger to fear? But Lila waited awake. They were in her care. Somehow she had to get help.

3

The Girl

The World Around lay at the southern end of Malham village, a long, low building with narrow windows and huge stone slates on the roof, pressing it down into the earth. Steve's father ran the bar downstairs; in summer, his mother ran the rest of the old place as a guest house – seven little rooms with views over the green hills and white rock of the Yorkshire Dales.

Steve didn't like his house invaded by strangers. He looked forward to the winter when the flow of guests all but dried up. The family had its own kitchen and sitting and dining rooms but the stairways and corridors were shared with guests. Steve often bumped into them as they came to and fro. The visitors were mainly walkers, climbers, potholers and the like. They tended to disdain the Tiger Park, only a few miles up the Dales from here. They thought it was a misuse of the National Park. But sometimes guests to the Tiger Park came to visit, and then Steve didn't mind how long they stayed. He could sit and talk tigers for hours. He knew the names and histories of every tiger in the park.

It was early spring. The real flood of visitors had not yet begun. There was only one couple staying – he'd seen them in the bar last night, steadily eating their way through steak pie and chips like a pair of earth movers on a building site. Steve despised walkers, who seemed to treat the countryside as a vast open air leisure centre, treading it behind them rather than treasuring it for the living things that made it their home. He'd glare at them if he met them in the corridor.

That was what he hated most about living in a guest house. Having to be polite to the invader.

Steve woke up this morning and immediately remembered the geography homework he'd left to do. He sat up and groaned. Then he rubbed his face, and went straight to the table where the books were spread out, waiting for him. It was due in that morning. He'd been late so often he'd get detention if it happened again.

He picked up a pencil, scratched his nose with the end of it, rubbed the sleep out of his eyes, and began to write.

Steve's small room on the first floor was plastered with pictures of rock stars and actors and animals, but mainly of tigers. He had posters of half the tigers in the park, including a magnificent one of Tiny, the biggest male, making a kill of a red deer stag. But his favourite picture was close to the head of his bed. Lila – the most beautiful and cleverest of the tigers, in his view. He believed – almost – that she was magic. He felt certain she knew him as well as he knew her.

Steve got through two pages of work before hunger suddenly attacked him. He had to get some cereal and a glass of milk before he ate his exercise book. He left the table, went to the door, opened it a fraction and waited a bit, listening.

The way was clear.

Steve slipped out of his room, closing the door

carefully behind him to hide it from prying eyes – the guests were always unpleasantly curious – and walked softly along the landing. He had to pass the room the walkers occupied. Hopefully they'd be out, pounding the hills flat.

The big clock above the dresser in the kitchen showed eight o'clock. Often his mother would be up by this time, cooking breakfast for the guests. But today there was no sign. She'd have made packed lunches for the two walkers. They'd be up and halfway to Hawes by this time.

Steve went to the front door. It was open. Typical – the walkers would have closed their own front door soon enough. He picked up a pint of cold milk from the step, punched down the silver cap and drank straight from the bottle, first the thick cream, then the milk. He drank half the bottle. Outside the cool air was pale and dim through a thick layer of grey cloud. It smelt of damp earth and rain, as usual. Steve looked down the length of the house and saw that the door to the barn was open, too.

The World Around had been a pub as long as anyone could remember, but the old building was built like a farmhouse with accommodation for people in one half of the building, and a barn in the other. Perhaps the landlords in past centuries had kept horses there. No doubt they kept a cow or two, as well, and pigs and chickens ran around the fields connected to the house.

These days the little field around the side and back of the pub was a beer garden with benches and chairs and swings and a slide for the kids. Chickens still scratched about, together with a few Muscovy ducks, more for show than for the eggs. The barn half of the building had been converted into more bedrooms. Only the last two or three metres of it was still a barn. There were bales of straw, old beer barrels and other jumble on the floor. There was a small hayloft with more bales of straw up in the roof. It was a handy storeroom. The only trouble was, they had to keep the door shut or the chickens got in and laid eggs you could never find, and the Muscovy ducks perched on the garden furniture and squirted all over it.

It really irritated Steve that the barn door was open. They – the guests – had been prying. Once, he'd come home and found all the things in his drawers rearranged. Nothing was gone, but everything had been taken out, examined, sniffed, probably, turned inside out and put back the wrong way by some wretched potholer. Now they had been prying in the barn, where they had no business to be.

Still clutching the milk bottle in his hand, Steve hurried grumpily along the mossy stone path that ran around the house. He was only a few steps away when he heard a noise from inside. He paused, uncertain. He really couldn't bring himself to tell the guests off for prying – it was too embarrassing. He stood still and peered into the shadows.

The door swung suddenly open and a girl ran out. Her skin was the colour of the dawn sky. She flung herself down at his feet. Steve shuffled back in a scare and the milk slopped in the bottle, some of it falling on her almost white hair and her half naked shoulder. The girl

43

leaned forward and seized his foot with a smooth rapid movement, and held it hard so he couldn't get away. She sank down on one knee, the other leg stretched out behind her and she leaned forward to press her forehead against his bare foot.

Steve stared down at her in horror. She was wearing nothing but an old blanket. Her shoulders were heaving in distress. The milk ran white against her astonishing skin. Her gesture was one of complete submission as if she were begging him for her life – or thanking him for it. She was panting as if she had run a mile, but he knew at once it wasn't that. This girl lived in terror.

Steve drew back his foot again, but she clung to it in desperation. 'What are you doing here?' he begged. Then, 'Do my parents know?'

But the girl didn't say a word. She lay as she was, gasping raggedly. She was begging. But for what?

'I have to fetch my parents,' began Steve. He tugged harder with his foot. The girl glanced up at him and he was terrified to see how her eyes rolled, how desperate she looked. It seemed that everything, life itself, depended on what he did.

Steve could bear it no longer. He kicked his foot violently away and jumped back. The girl rose to her knees, clutched her two hands together and shook them as if in prayer.

'Aha. Aha,' she said. Steve glanced involuntarily over his shoulder, worried that his parents might catch him in this strange encounter. What on earth was going on? Did this girl seriously think she could stay here without anyone knowing? What did she want?

The girl had turned and was crawling on all fours back into the barn. She peered out at him and put a finger to her lips. Her meaning was clear. Hush. Don't say a word. Don't tell anyone that I'm here.

Steve was over the worst of his fright now, although his heart was still pounding. She was the strangest thing he had ever seen; her skin was white and grey and pale rose, but she was only a girl after all, a slightly built girl. She was a few years older than him, a little bigger. She appeared to be naked under the blanket wrapped around her shoulders, which he thought he recognised as one he had seen before, lying around in the barn. Her nakedness scared him, although he couldn't help trying to peer and see her body under the blanket. She was beautiful and exciting. She looked as if she could be very strong.

She must have escaped from a psychiatric hospital. Yes, she was mad. But there were no psychiatric hospitals anywhere near that he knew of. Her cheekbones were high, her eyes were slightly slanted, almost Chinese. Definitely not European. She could almost have been an American Indian, but for her pale skin and her bright hair. which was almost the same colour as her skin. She crouched on all fours, slowly peering this way and that. As he watched, she lifted her head and sniffed the air. She was perfectly astonishing.

The girl gestured that he was to come closer, that he was to come into the barn with her. She had something to show him ...? She beckoned with her finger and tried to smile but it was a poor ghost of a smile. Steve noticed now that she was shivering violently. She was slight and so humble it was difficult to be scared of her. Even so, he didn't want to go into the dark barn. There might be other people waiting there.

The girl smiled again and moved deeper into the shadows inside. She gestured inside.

'Wait here,' Steve told her firmly. 'I'll get you some clothes and stuff.'

He turned and ran. He had a glimpse of the girl sinking to her knees and holding out her arms imploringly, but he wasn't going to give her away – yet. Obviously he had to tell; he could scarcely hide a stranger in his house. But his mum and dad were probably still in bed; they never got up till the last minute, because of their late nights with the pub. He didn't need to wake them yet. The girl looked so helpless. He'd get her some clothes. He was secretly interested in her nakedness but it was quite impossible to deal with her like that. And she needed something to eat and drink first. Then he could try to find out what was going on. Then he'd get some help ...

As he ran into the house, Steve decided that the girl *must* be mad. It was obvious. She couldn't speak. She didn't seem to know or care that she was wearing next to nothing. But where on earth could she have come from? Perhaps she had been kept in secret by someone in the village, and had never seen the light of day. She must have escaped. Or perhaps she had been a stowaway from some far-off country. But what country produced people with that bright pale skin, the colour of the air, and slanted eyes?

Steve ran around the house collecting clothes. It was

a bit awkward, he couldn't go and empty the drawers because anything missing would be noticed. He ended up going into the old clothes bags and came up with a pair of underpants, a pair of his mum's tights, an old shirt, a cardigan and a short black skirt from his Aunt Jenny, a tiny woman who sometimes came to stay. Then he collected food from the kitchen and hurried back to the barn.

He was beginning to enjoy this. He hoped the clothes would fit. He'd probably get a reward or something for helping her – or for giving her up.

Back at the barn he got nervous again. He wouldn't go in; he threw the clothes in through the door. The girl had been hiding among the garden furniture, but now she came out and gathered the clothes silently to herself and watched him. Steve peered inside. It seemed to be all right. He took a couple of steps in and smiled nervously. It smelt odd in there. He couldn't place the smell, although he'd smelt it before, but he knew it was very out of place. It was very quiet. He stayed close to the door.

'Put them on, then,' he told her. 'Here, I've got you some food as well.' He shook the carrier bag at her. The girl stared, not understanding. 'Get dressed, you're cold,' he said again. He mimed pulling the clothes on. The girl nodded and did as she was told.

The girl had been deadly serious so far, but once she started getting the clothes on, she changed completely. She began by pulling up the tights. She looked anxiously at Steve to see if she was doing the right thing. He was looking the other way; the blanket had dropped to the floor. She called to him, 'Aha? Aha?' and he glanced quickly at her and nodded. Yes, she was doing the right thing. She wasn't very used to tights. They ended up in bags and rolls round her knees and ankles. They were too big anyway. She looked down at her legs, put her hand to her mouth and giggled. She looked absurd – completely ridiculous!

Next were the underpants. He tried to explain they went under and not over the tights, but she was having a good time. He'd thought they were his but they turned out to be an old pair of his dad's. Mr Hattersly was rather fat. The girl chuckled to herself and grinned. She pulled them up high. They reached almost to her armpits.

Steve felt a lot better now she was covered up. He rocked with laughter as the girl, grinning madly, made a parade around the barn with the tights sticking out of the bottom of the underpants, which were under her armpits and full of holes and hung off her in folds. She waved her hand in the air and stuck her bottom out at a jaunty angle. She was really funny. Then she got the shirt on. She was stuck with the buttons; Steve had to help her do them up. He felt embarrassed, with his fingers grazing the skin on her stomach as he fiddled with the silly little things from the wrong way round.

The little black skirt from Aunt Jenny was microscopic – the girl was a good four inches taller than his aunt. It didn't even cover the bottom of her bum, although it didn't matter since that was covered by the tights and underpants. The cardigan was Jenny's too, a little tank top that came just below her ribs. The overall

48

effect was ridiculous – but also, somehow, slightly fashionable-looking. She only wanted a few rings in her nose and ears and her hair cut short and she would have been a proper teen-dream.

The girl was performing a strange little jig around the barn, posing with her hands up in the air and rolling her eyes. Then she jumped right up in the air and landed in a handstand with her clothes around her ears and grinned at him, until Steve was groaning with laughter.

Suddenly he remembered his parents – someone might come by. 'Sssh!' he said suddenly. The girl glanced at the door, then anxiously up towards the hayloft.

Steve followed her eye. 'What's up there?' he asked curiously. The girl looked at him thoughtfully but made no move to show him. She started picking through the rest of the clothes instead.

Steve had certainly picked the worst possible clothes, but she seemed delighted by them. She found another pair of tights and made Steve try them on. He wasn't such a clown as she was; he stood in the barn with them taut over his pyjamas feeling self conscious, while she fell about, slapping the floor with amusement and trying to giggle silently.

Steve thought, maybe she wasn't a nutcase after all. He wondered if she was a refugee from one of those tyrannical regimes. If the authorities caught her she'd get sent back and shot. Perhaps he would keep her secret after all ...

He took out the food: a jam jar with the lid screwed tightly on full of milk, some bananas, an apple, some bread and a few cold sausages left over from guests' breakfasts. His mother saved them for the cat or the dog, but Steve often stole them. The girl devoured two of the sausages, sticking them into her mouth with no manners at all. She popped the others down her front and patted them with a smile. Steve assumed they were for later. Then she picked up a banana and tried to eat it without taking the skin off. Steve had to slap his hand over his mouth to stop laughing. He showed her how to peel it.

'Don't they have bananas where you come from?' he wanted to know. She peeled it with concentration and then ate delicately, smiling at him with her white teeth and kicking her heels against the bale of straw.

'Steven!' It was his mother. She had found he was not in bed. It was late.

Steve jumped up and went to the door. 'I won't tell,' he said impulsively. The girl stood up. She held out her hands and then pointed upwards. She beckoned; there was something up in the hayloft after all, and she wanted him to see it.

He glanced nervously up. Were there more of them? But it was too late to see, anyway. 'I have to go,' he said.

She stared at him, serious again. He had no idea how much she understood. She hadn't said a thing, not a word in any language. Suddenly she ran forward a few steps, so quickly she was on him before he knew she was moving. She flung her arms around him and held him tightly and buried her face in his neck. Steve put his arms on her waist. She held him for several seconds, binding him to her. Then she let go and stepped back.

'But you can't stay here for long, you can see that, can't you?' he said nervously. The girl stared at him. His mother called again. Steve smiled uncertainly, closed the door, and ran back into the house.

On the way to school, Steve began to have doubts. Despite her fun, the girl must be in some dreadful kind of trouble. Earlier, she had seemed to be begging him for her life. Was her life something he could give her? He was thinking about this in the playground before school, when Alison Savey came up to him and asked eagerly, 'Did you hear about the Tiger Park?'

Steve had been too busy to hear or watch the news. But most of the other kids knew all about it.

By all accounts, it had been a massacre – of men and tigers. Not all the details were available – the attack had only been discovered a few hours ago – but over the course of the morning more news came through. By lunchtime, the whole school knew everything.

The guards and Park workers had been tied up and drugged. None of them knew anything about it. There had been a truck, and it was assumed the poachers had removed the tigers to this once they were dead and then taken them away to sell for the Chinese bone trade. But something had gone terribly wrong ...

Eight dead tigers were still lying in or near their cages. And not far off, mauled to death by their would-be victims, lay five dead men. Judging from the pug marks they had found in the fields around the enclosure, some of the cats at least had managed to escape and were currently at large.

Tragically, the dead body of one of the Park workers, Nicky Abbot, had been found just outside the holding block, dead, with a bullet in his head. Nicky had been on duty that night. The most likely theory was that he had escaped and tried to raise the alarm, and that the poachers had killed him. In the ensuing chaos some of the tigers had escaped. The poachers had panicked and fled.

Everyone was stunned by the news. Malham Tiger Park had not been universally popular. Some had welcomed it for the money it brought to the area, some because it was such an important conservation project. But others had been fearful – farmers for their livestock, others for the safety of the community, should the tigers escape. Still, the Park was the biggest thing that had ever happened in that part of the world. Everyone was horrified that such a thing could happen in their safe, quiet little village. The wholesale slaughter of these magnificent animals, already so near to extinction. Six dead men, five of them killed by the tigers who, everybody had been assured over and over, were perfectly safe. As for Nicky Abbot, he lived in nearby Grassington and was known and liked locally. The whole thing was awful.

Steve passed the day in a state of shock. He had taken more of an interest in the tigers than anyone. Everyone knew he was the local expert. He saw people watching him, trying to work out what emotions he must be feeling. He just felt sick. He'd almost rather die than have to get through this day. The tigers had been his world. He knew them like friends.

Later in the morning, Dale, the boy who sat next to him, nodded out of the window. There was a policeman standing outside the railings of the playground. And another, further along, and another couple up by the gates. Steve stared: there was something odd about them. Then he realised. They were armed.

'What do they want guns for?' he whispered.

'Hunting the tigers, I expect,' replied Dale. Steve could hardly believe it – as if it was people who had anything to fear! Wasn't it obvious? The whole story was the other way round.

He was so shocked that it was hours before he suddenly remembered the girl. Of course – she must have something to do with this! She must have a part in it ... And then Steve forgot the fun of the morning. He began to hate her with a fierce, bright hatred. She must be one of the poachers. What other explanation was there? If that was the case, he would hand her over to the police with the very greatest of pleasure.

At the same time – such a young girl – she couldn't be more than fourteen, she didn't even appear to have any language – could she really be involved with anything so desperate? The thing was, you couldn't take the chance. The poachers had to be caught and punished.

Steve was on the verge of putting up his hand to tell his teacher, Mrs Pickles, when he was overtaken by events.

It was shortly before afternoon break that one of the girls, Sandra Winters, began to cry. Mrs Pickles led her out. Left without an adult in the class, a couple of other children began to weep. For the first time, Steve noticed how pale everyone looked. A sense of panic was spreading around the class. It was partly a feeling that if something so terrible could happen just up the road, couldn't it happen here? Murder – massacre? But more than that – there were tigers on the loose. There was the proof: policemen on the streets with guns. The tigers had killed. They were in hiding. They could be anywhere. They could be in the school! They could be waiting at home ...

Mrs Pickles came back into the class and explained that the armed men were not there to hunt the tigers, but to protect the children on the way home, if necessary. Although she hardly thought it would be necessary. All the experts were agreed that the tigers would stay far away from human habitation. However, as a safety precaution it would be better for everyone to go home quickly and remain inside. The police would be there to escort them to their houses. Mrs Pickles was in no doubt that the tigers would be captured, and quickly, hopefully with anaesthetic darts.

'We shall be resuming normal service as soon as possible,' smiled Mrs Pickles. 'And now – I think we can all do with going home a little early, don't you?'

There was a TV camera filming them coming out of the school gates. Steve's best friend, Guy, wanted him to come back to his place to watch the news, but he wouldn't. He hurried home, past the burly policemen who seemed to be standing every few metres on every street. No doubt any one of them would love to kill a tiger.

All Steve wanted to do now was to clear his home of that girl, who he was certain had been at the Tiger Park last night. She was stained with their blood.

4

Men and Dogs

But when he reached the green just outside his house, the way was already barred. A crowd had gathered on the road before his house. Something had just happened, word was just now spreading. People were running down the road to see, calling to each other. And policemen everywhere – talking on their radios, trying to push people back, policemen running, pointing, giving and receiving orders. As he watched, a police car and a van drew up and more policemen jumped out. They immediately began trying to get people to move away from The World Around, which stood deserted and alone amongst the quickly growing crowd.

Steve tried to move forward but he was pushed back with the others. Now, a Tiger Park Land-Rover drew up; Park Rangers jumped out carrying rifles loaded with darts. Steve could see Mike Craven, the Director of the Park, push his way across the green and grab hold of a senior officer. Other policemen were now clambering up onto roofs and appearing at windows of nearby houses. They were training their rifles onto his house.

Steve was filled with a sudden panic – something had happened at his house. What about his parents ...?

Again, he tried to push forward at the rope but a policeman stopped him.

'You can't go through here, son, it's dangerous.'

'But I live here!'

The big man peered down at him. 'The World Around?' he said.

'Yes,' said Steve indignantly.

'Name?'

'Steven Hattersly.'

The policeman peered across the heads of the gathering crowd. People were coming in from all directions. The village was already swollen with sightseers after the massacre. Now they were all heading into the centre of the action, and the police just weren't ready for them.

'Sergeant ... Sergeant ... Hang on a minute, son, I'll find someone to take care of you.' As he spoke, Steve saw his mother in the crowd. The policeman got her attention and she burst through the wedge of people, ran up to him and took him in her arms. Steve shook her off.

'What's going on?' he demanded.

'The tigers,' she explained. She glanced up at the house, her house, now inaccessible, dangerous. 'One minute I was doing the dishes. The next I was surrounded by policemen with loudspeakers and dogs and rifles. I felt like Al Capone.'

'What happened?' demanded Steve angrily. His mother was rambling on again. She always made a story out of everything, without telling him a thing he wanted to know.

'I told you,' she said. 'They found the tigers hiding in our barn. They're still there. They're going to try and get them out now.'

Behind them someone began to call through a loudspeaker. 'Clear the streets! This is an emergency.

57

There is a roadblock at the other end of the village; if you go behind the roadblock we will be able to protect you. You are in danger here. This is a police operation and there is danger. Please ... clear the streets ... clear the streets...'

Steve said, 'But there was a girl in there this morning. I didn't see any tigers.'

'You must give your men orders not to shoot to kill.'

Inspector Willis could have struck the man to one side in impatience. People had got past the roadblocks before he could even set them up. Now there was a growing crowd, dogs barking, people shouting, all within a few yards of the bloody tigers. It was an extremely dangerous situation and it was his job to get it under control. Now he had this idiot to deal with. But he merely said, 'You know I can't do that, sir. There's a danger to human life. That's my responsibility.'

'There's no danger ...'

'Tell that to those Chinese we found today.'

Mike Craven groaned in frustration. In ten years not one of the tigers had ever tried to attack a guard. But there was no denying the killing of men at the Tiger Park the night before, or that the two men found on the tops above Malham Cove during the course of the day had been killed by a tiger. He had been called upon to identify the wounds. He had even recognised the pug marks. Lila – of all of them, the one you would least expect to turn against man.

The policeman pushed off through the crowd but Mike ran after him. He had to jostle through the crowd, which was getting thicker and thicker. A group of journalists had found the officer too. Camera crews were dragging their equipment through the crowd, pursuing both Mike and Willis, trying to get a few comments.

Mike reached through the crowd and grabbed the officer by the shoulder and dragged him round. Willis swung round, infuriated.

'Do you want me to get you taken in?' he hissed.

'Look – I'm sorry,' begged Mike, 'but these animals are right on the edge of extinction. The tigers in that barn represent a chance to start again. At least give my men with the darts the chance to shoot first ...'

Inspector Willis was furious. 'Look, if you really want to help yourself and us and the tigers, do something to clear this crowd. Now if you harass me again I'll have you taken in. Understand?'

The crowd was so big now it had completely overwhelmed the police, who had been spread out all over the Dales looking for clues. No one had expected the tigers to hide inside a village. Ropes had been put up to cordon the area off, but they were being pushed down. Willis glared disgustedly at a big Rottweiler barking loudly near his feet.

'If one of your tigers comes running out into this lot, my men will have to shoot. I'll get into a damn sight worse trouble for a dead child than a dead tiger, I promise you.'

A journalist swung a microphone under Mike's nose. 'What do you have to say about the two dead men found at Malham Cove?' he demanded. 'Did you know you had a potential man-eater in the Park before this happened?'

'She didn't eat him, she just killed him,' snapped Mike. The journalists glanced at each other and laughed.

'Well, I 'ope those two fellers appreciate it, it were very nice of tiger to leave summat to bury,' said someone.

'What do you have to say to critics who claim this shows that the Tiger Park should never have been sited here?'

'Were they Triad members, Inspector?' shouted another at the policeman's retreating back.

Mike ignored the questions and tried to crane himself up above the heads of the crowd.

'Please go back ... go back!' he bawled. 'If the tigers come out now the police will shoot them ... we want to try and save the tigers ...'

It was no use. The racket was so loud no one could hear him. There was a policeman nearby with a loudspeaker. He seemed to have given up getting the crowd back and was joking with a young woman. Steve leaned across and tried to snatch the loudspeaker out of his hand. But the policeman pulled it back irritably. It was his loudspeaker. He wasn't going to give his loudspeaker to no civilians.

A couple of motorbikes drew up. The dogs were barking their heads off; they could smell the tigers in the barn. People seemed drunk; the whole thing had taken on a fairground atmosphere.

A dog slipped its lead and made a run at the barn,

60

barking furiously. From within there was a ferocious snarl and the barn door trembled from some tremendous blow within.

The crowd watched in shock in the sudden silence that followed. The dog tucked its tail between its legs and fled. Someone screamed. Suddenly everyone understood that there was a big predator only metres away. They began to shuffle backwards, jamming up against those at the back who, feeling safe behind the wall of people, were pushing forward. Then, a flash of orange appeared in the gaps of wood in the door. Shouts, more screams from the crowd. The door of the barn shook as some huge creature lashed at it. The planks of old oak, an inch thick, began to splinter. People began to fall and stampede in their hurry to get away; the dogs began to howl.

Mike made another go for the loudspeaker. He held it to his mouth and yelled as loudly as he could, holding the irate policeman off with one hand as he did so.

'Please clear the streets,' he begged. 'Clear the streets or the police will shoot ... The tigers are safe if you stand back. We have to save the tigers ...'

As he spoke another dog made a dash at the barn. In answer the great barn door shook, crumpled and burst apart. The tiger emerged like a demon as the door disintegrated and destroyed the dog in an explosion of orange and black and shattered wood.

Lila had been waiting for the dogs all day. She understood how they tracked. She could disguise her scent, but Donna and Will were impossible.

Lila understood a good many things. She knew, for example, the difference between a gun and a dart rifle, although since the previous night that difference meant a good deal less. She knew the boy was friendly. She could make him hers if she wanted but she could not tell him anything. Perhaps if she had shown him the tigers hidden in the hayloft – but how would he have known what she wanted when she didn't know herself what to do?

She had tried to make Donna and Will understand that they should be quiet but as the day went on they were getting restless and hungry. She lay staring at the chickens through the gaps in the stone slates on the roof, but the birds were so stupid it was impossible to get them to do anything. In the late afternoon Will began to prowl about, growling and complaining. The boards creaked under his weight. Lila, crouching low, approached him and licked his muzzle. He was placated and lay down next to her. But for how long?

When the dogs came she knew the end was near.

Dogs ran with men. Her lip curled silently as she first heard them, then saw them – the police tracker dogs following her scent down from the hills, where they had found the dead men. The dogs lifted their heads as they got near the barn and barked wildly. Then the policemen came. To make sure they slipped the lead of one of the dogs, who ran in. Will roared, the frustration of the day pouring out of him. The dog ran, tail between its legs. The men backed off and prepared their rifles.

It would happen very fast now.

A quick run around showed Lila that there was no way out. They already had the place surrounded. She knew at once that the only thing to do was to lie still, to be calm, to show no danger, present no threat. Then they might use the dart guns. But that was impossible! Hard enough for her – but for Donna? And Will ...? A tiger wasn't made to lie like a rabbit in its hide. It wasn't that they wanted to harm the men – why should they? Only Lila had a taste for revenge.

The fear of the men transformed her. Now she sat, an arm around each tiger's neck, squeezing tight. It was dangerous – neither of them really understood who she was, it was possible they could turn on her. She pulled hard at Will's neck. He was twisting his head and snarling. Any minute now he'd make a run for it.

Outside was already thick with people shouting, pushing, dogs barking. At one point Lila heard the voice of Mike Craven and she felt a flash of hope. Nicky Abbot had betrayed her – surely not Mike as well? But even if he was on her side he was only one; the others were so many. And Lila knew very well how people feared her species.

A dog was barking close up to the door. Someone started to shout through a loudspeaker. Donna snarled, shook Lila off, paced two or three times in front of the door. She struck at it with her paw; Lila heard the shock of the people outside as they understood what they were contending with. Donna turned to look at Lila, her lips curled back, her ears back, her eyes narrow. She would charge any second. Lila was transformed back to herself. Will rose to his feet. In a swift movement he ran to the door and peered out. There was a fusillade of barking and shouting at the sight of his face.

Lila ran to the door, pushed him aside and barred the way. If she could talk she would have cried, 'Stay here ... it's safe here ... stay here ...' But she couldn't speak and the noise outside was terrific.

Now Will asserted himself. He had done as she wanted all day but now the hour was his. He curled back his lips. Lila had only one chance – she took it. She seized the big male by the eye. She could do it easily enough. She saw his jaw open, his face droop. But ... Lila could have wept with shame. This was her superior; she had no right.

She could not carry it through.

She released Will and lay down on her side. Will recovered and walked up to her, bent his face down to her so that she could lick his muzzle submissively. Then he lifted his head and sniffed the air outside.

A dog came rushing at the barn and with a great roar, Will leapt forward and struck the barn door with his paw. Under his weight it crushed and he went charging through, scattering beams and splintered wood. At once there was a crack of gunshot, then the hiss of a dart. Lila heard Mike shouting, 'Leave him ... leave him, I got him with a dart.' But there was another shot all the same, and then another and another, just to make sure. People were screaming and fighting, getting trampled underfoot in their efforts to get away.

Now Donna panicked. She made a couple of little runs at the door, and then rushed outside and in seconds was in amongst the seething mass of people.

More gunfire; then again. Lila had lost everything; there was only herself to save.

She was transformed. She jumped lightly back up to the hayloft where there was a small opening into the loft of the house – far too small for Donna or Will, even if they had been willing. But she could squeeze in easily enough.

Inside the dusty attic space, Lila ran until she found the opening down into the house. She opened the trapdoor, dropped down, replaced it. She ran along and peeped out of an upstairs window. She could see Will lying on his side, motionless. Donna was some way off, also down, but with her head up, still snarling. Mike Craven was standing before her with his arms outstretched, trying to protect her.

She could never escape from here. Perhaps the other side of the building ...

Lila ran round. Here too, there was no way forward. There were people everywhere. As soon as she left the house she would be amongst people and then men with rifles would get her. If she went out as she was, transformed, they would catch her and ask her questions she could not understand, let alone answer.

Unless ... if she was right among the people ... if she could get quickly into the crowd ... Maybe then they would not dare to shoot. She understood something of the terror these people had of killing their own kind.

Lila opened the window and prepared to leap from the first floor window directly into the crowd.

The tiger appeared like magic from the wrong side of the house.

It was impossible – there was no way for such a big

65

animal to get across from the barn to the house with no one seeing. It seemed to flicker on, almost, as it descended from the window and suddenly it was there right where it should not be, right in amongst the crowd, the thing everyone dreaded. At once, screams, terror, total panic. The gunmen on the roof pointed their rifles, but men, women and children were running before and behind the beast, everyone was running – they would certainly have hit someone.

Inspector Willis ran forward, shouting, 'Watch it! Watch the bloody thing ...!' He could see it swatting at people with its claws. God knows what damage it was doing, snarling like a demon. The men were waiting for a gap to fire into but it was running right in the thickest part of the crowd. It seemed to be herding the poor wretches like sheep. This was his worst nightmare. He began to wave his arms to attract attention.

'Shoot! Shoot!' he screamed. So what if someone was hit by a bullet? It could hardly be worse than this. His men heard him, but they couldn't bring themselves to do it.

The big cat spun and ran, always in the thick of the crowd. It was enormous. Its roars filled the little village, mingled with screams of terror. It had chased the people into a tight mass, cringing away from it against the wall of a house. Now at last the marksmen would get a clear sight; but the tiger paused, spun on its haunches ... and leapt right into the thick of the crowd.

Margot Hattersly was among the people chivvied by the tiger. She tried running every way she could; she kept

66

dodging and leaping but it was always there like some terrible party trick, always right behind her. It was livid with rage and power. She had been swatted two or three times by the great paws as she ran, but she felt nothing – shock, she supposed. She'd be bleeding to death in half an hour. Then, suddenly, there was nowhere to run. She was on her knees, her hands held uselessly over her head, as the great cat swung with grace and leapt directly at her in a single liquid movement. She felt the weight of it bludgeon into her and waited for death.

She was gasping on her hands and knees. Where was the hot breath, the teeth around her neck, which was as fragile as a straw? She looked cautiously up.

There was nothing.

She raised her head higher. People were running in all directions, staring wildly this way and that. The tiger was nowhere to be seen. She peered around her. Nothing. Nothing. Nothing.

In front of her was a girl, grinning at her. The girl whooped. Mrs Hattersly passed a hand over her eyes weakly. The girl was extraordinary. Her skin looked daubed with some bizarre make-up. She was wearing a tiny black dress, a pair of tights full of holes, and over them – Mrs Hattersly was quite certain about this because the skirt flipped up when the girl whooped – was a pair of baggy men's underpants.

'Underpants as a fashion accessory,' she muttered. She glanced around her again, in a sudden panic, but the tiger really had vanished into thin air. Must have run off while she was on her hands and knees in the road. Her knees were beginning to hurt her. She got up. She remembered the swatting she had received and began patting herself all over to find how badly she had been mauled.

The girl was standing right in front of her laughing wildly at her bemused expression. She was almost glad she wasn't young any more, if that's what you had to wear. What's more, the underpants looked exactly like an old pair of her husband's. She'd have to let him know – he was in fashion at last!

The girl ran off down the road. Mrs Hattersly continued patting herself all over to find the wounds she was convinced must be all over her. But despite the fact she was certain the tiger had got her several times, there was nothing ... just a few bruises where the huge soft paws, the claws sheathed, had batted her in the right direction.

She looked up to see her husband hurrying into the bar. It was probably the safest place after all. He turned at the door and shouted, 'Bar open!' at the top of his voice.

Immediately a great stream of people were buffeting her as they thronged towards the pub. Well, Al was a lousy businessman, but he always had an eye for the good chance. Mrs Hattersly ran with the crowd. She needed a stiff drink herself.

The girl ran round behind the house. Out of sight she paused, unsure of where to go and how to hide. She was drawn to the long house because of the boy. She climbed in at a window and found herself standing in the kitchen, although she had no idea what sort of room it was. She tried to hide in the cupboards but they were all too full.

At one end of the room was a huge ancient fireplace. There was a set of shelves in it these days to store pots and pans, but the throat was still open, leading to the wide chimney of years gone by. No one would ever find her there!

Chuckling to herself for her cleverness, the girl climbed up into the sooty darkness. After a couple of metres she found a ledge, and here she sat, in complete darkness. It felt very safe.

Shortly, she began to weep silently.

5

Man Killer

After the two tigers had been taken away and the crowd had dispersed, the police put the village under curfew and conducted a thorough search. It was of great importance that Lila, of all the tigers, was swiftly captured. All the evidence suggested that it was she who had killed the Triad men at the Tiger Park the night before as well as the two men found mauled to death over Malham Cove. It was a miracle she hadn't injured anyone during her run through the village.

Four hundred police officers combed every inch of the barn, the roads, the fields around the village and the hills around the fields. They found nothing.

Lila had disappeared into thin air.

Steve spent an hour that night being questioned about the girl by the police. They used a photo identity kit and ended up with a picture that looked very like her. Later, the Hattersly family, like so many others in Malham that night, huddled around the TV set and watched their adventure played out on the television news.

The curfew was lifted overnight and early the next morning Steve went round to the barn to have a look for himself.

Everything seemed as it always had done. It was difficult to imagine that there had been three tigers hiding in it the day before, even more difficult to imagine that he had been watching a strange girl dress up and clown around while the big cats hid and watched them, silently, from the hayloft.

Had the girl known? What was her connection with the tigers? Somehow, Steve found it hard to believe she was their enemy.

Up in the hayloft, rubbed off on the wood, were a number of short, bright, orange and black hairs – all there was to show that he had been visited by these fiercest of all carnivores.

Steve peered down from the hayloft. He was where the tigers had been. They had been watching him. He remembered what the policeman who had interviewed him had said.

'You were lucky,' he'd said. 'Lila must have left before you came along. The other two are evidently safe enough, but that one – she's a devil. The sooner she's caught, the better.'

He looked down at Steve's anxious face. 'You'll be all right, though, old son; you'll be having an armed guard around your house tonight. I don't suppose she'll come back. But – just in case.'

'But who was the girl?' asked Steve.

'That's what we'd like to know,' said the policeman.

A chicken squeezed through the open door and ran in, peering about in the gloom. Looking for a place to lay her egg, thought Steve. He watched it peer around into an old tea chest. He imagined that he was the tiger, and the innocent, foolish chicken was him. He could scare it half to death just by shouting 'boo'...

Steve's thoughts were disturbed by the door to the

71

barn opening suddenly. A group of strangers came in. They had a camera with them and a huge, woolly microphone.

'Hey – who are you? What d'you think you're doing up there?' barked one of them when he saw Steve hiding up above.

'I live here,' said Steve coldly. 'Who are you?'

'Oh – Steven – you must be Steven ...' The man smiled at him, nice all of a sudden. 'We're from the telly – we're filming for the news. Mind if we have a word with you? It's quite an adventure you've had ...'

The media had discovered Malham. By evening the rooms at The World Around and every other guest house were full of journalists and camera teams from the TV and the national newspapers. The Tiger Park massacre was the biggest story in the world.

Later that day, TV cameras followed white-faced children trotting nervously down the pavements and in through the school gates. Policemen cradling firearms escorted them on their way. For a little while the streets were busy and normal. But when all the children were safely in school, it became clear that people were taking police advice and staying inside. The armed police who waited on every corner had no one to protect.

There was fear in Malham. Not of the Triad, who had slaughtered the tigers and probably committed murder so nearby. The terror was Lila.

The escaped tigress began to exercise a strange power over people's imaginations, but it was difficult to pin down exactly what this was. She was called a man-eater, although in fact she had not touched the bodies of any of her victims. It was more than that. It was understandable that she had killed those men at the Tiger Park – they had been attacking her after all. But carefully to track down and kill the two who had fled across the hills ... Was that the act of animal? Why had she done that? Not for food. Not because of any immediate danger.

What kind of an animal was it that sought revenge?

And another thing – where on earth had she gone? There were helicopters over the Dales, trained dogs, hordes of officers and experts with a small mountain of equipment. How was it that Lila could evade them all so easily? Her pug marks were everywhere – all around the hills above the Tiger Park, by the cove where the two men had been killed on the night of the massacre, in the village, in the barn at The World Around. She had been seen again by any number of eyewitnesses harrying the crowd in Malham the day the tigers had been tracked to the barn. It should have been an easy job to hunt down such a distinctive animal. The ground was wet; it was impossible for even a rabbit to cross the fields without leaving some mark.

Journalists at first ignored the eyewitness accounts of the tiger disappearing into thin air that day she had been cornered with Will and Donna Bella in Malham. They assumed that fright and the speed of the big cat had confused people. But later that day, when it became obvious that the police were at a complete loss as to where she had gone, they began to tell tales. The tiger was turning into a myth.

The fear grew, the stories spread – how Lila didn't need to hunt but could command the sheep to come to her just by looking at them. How she sought revenge for her kind, for all of nature. How she appeared and disappeared like mist as it suited her. How she had a human girl as her consort – a human girl with eyes as orange as a tiger's, who left footprints at the scene of the crime painted red with the blood of the dead man, Nicky Abbot.

Where would the tigress appear next?

What did she want?

All that day the hunt for Lila lasted – with dogs, with helicopters, with search parties. Not a trace was found – not a whisker, not a scent, not a mark.

That evening the streets of Malham were empty.

Every newspaper, every television station in the wide world seemed to descend on Malham and half of them wanted an interview with Steve. Apart from the fact that he lived in the house where the tigers had been found and had spoken to the mysterious girl, they all soon found out he had a crush on the tigers. Steve enjoyed being a celebrity – for about two hours.

The microphones shoved in his face, the endless questions about the same thing, the prying into how he felt – pretty soon Steve had had enough. His father organised a press conference so they could all get it over with in one go. It was held in the pub in the afternoon with the whole family answering questions. He watched it on telly later the same night.

After that, Steve hoped they'd leave him alone, but they didn't. Immediately they were back onto him. Press conferences were all very well, but they wanted something the others hadn't heard and they were prepared to keep nagging and chasing till he provided it. Next day they even tracked him down in his room, pushing the door open and creeping in when his mother wasn't looking.

'Go away!' He was furious – they weren't even guests.

'It's all right, son, it's all right, calm down, we only want a word ...'

But it wasn't all right. Steve had really had enough. He pushed past them, through the door and along the corridors, and outside into the quiet village streets, anywhere he could be alone with his own thoughts.

He walked along the grass-edged village road, trying to ignore the dozen or so police or journalists eyeing him curiously. He couldn't see a single soul he knew.

'Does your mother know you're out on your own?' asked one policeman, in a well-meaning way.

'Of course she does,' sniffed Steve. The man watched him thoughtfully as he went up the road. There was a policeman on every corner. Along by the beck, a TV crew was filming the ducks for want of anything better. Steve turned off behind a house before they spotted him.

What he really wanted to do – what he was dying to do – was to go for a walk on the hills. But he was too scared. Lila was up there; she'd already killed seven men. Experts on the TV had emphasised how, once they had tasted human flesh, the big cats quickly got a taste for it. Steve remembered how the young tigress had caught him with her eye, made him bow his head and sink to his knees. All she had to do was catch sight of him from her hiding place among the rocks ...

Had she been practising that day? Somehow, at the time, it had been as if she was playing with him, joking and showing off. She was saying, Look! See what I can do!

Playing with him ... As a cat plays with a mouse?

He mooched along, hands in pockets trying to keep out of sight. He turned another corner – and walked right into yet another TV crew, a woman and two men. Their faces lit up when they saw him; they'd been searching all morning for a local resident out on the streets to interview.

The woman came jogging towards him. Behind her, two men hurriedly picked up their gear and came quickly after her, dragging camera and sound gear with them.

Steve fled.

'Hey ... just a minute,' shouted the woman. But Steve never stopped. At that moment he'd have fed her to the tiger if he could.

In the end he went into the bar, which was buzzing with people, in strange contrast to the empty streets. Half the village seemed to be there and loads of journalists as well. But in here they didn't seem to be so bothered about getting a story. They just joked and drank and talked shop with each other, and treated the locals as if they had disappeared as soon as they left the street.

His dad beamed at him across the bar and handed him a Coke and a packet of crisps.

'We're making a fortune,' he confided. 'I'm thinking of changing name o' pub to "Tiger". What d'yer reckon?'

Steve grinned. His father looked so pleased with life. He drank the Coke, and then wandered into the kitchen behind the bar, where his mother was furiously cutting sandwiches.

'Give us a hand, slice some cheese, Steven,' she groaned. 'I'll have to get in some extra help, I'm a drowning woman!'

Steve picked up the cheese slice and sat himself down at the workspace. 'What about Sue?' he asked.

'She's working this afternoon, but she'll be in this evening. I'll have put mesel' into a sandwich and served mesel' up by that time,' she said hollowly.

Steve laughed; she grinned. 'How's it going?' she asked.

'Pesky journalists,' said Steve gloomily.

'They always seem so nice on telly, don't they?'

'I can't get away from 'em.'

'They'll get bored soon, find summat else to write about. Make hay while sun shines, your father says.'

Steve shrugged and drew the sharp blade across the cheese, so that it fell away in clean slices. They stood working together until his mother finished an order and ran out to find her customer.

'Tomatas – I need tomatas,' she called back.

'Areet.'

As Steve picked up a sharp knife and began slicing tomatoes a wolf howled loudly just behind him.

Steve shot out of his seat, nicking his finger on the tomato knife. He looked wildly around. A wolf, in the kitchen? The howling had been so clear and loud he jumped up onto the table and peered this way and that, trying to spot the animal. Of course there was nothing there. Then he suddenly felt like a fool. A wolf, I ask you ...! Must be his nerves. You often got strange noises from drunk people in the bar.

He had heard that cry many times before, on radio or TV. But this had been so loud! He had almost felt its breath on his neck.

He picked up his knife again and started shakily on another tomato, but he had hardly got started when he heard it again. The wolf was definitely only metres away from him, howling terribly. This time he was certain it was in the room with him, but he was scared to run in case he went straight into it. But where? In the cupboards? He thought nervously of looking in the pantry, but a low growl made him sure he didn't want to.

Had someone got a telly on nearby? Or the radio? He checked, but the radio was off. Anyway, this had been too loud and clear for a radio. It'd had a hollow, echoing quality to it, but it sounded more real than anything he had heard on the telly.

Steve began cautiously to tiptoe towards the door. Then, an owl hooted at him. Steve spun around. It was ... ? The wolf growled mockingly and a bird laughed at him. Definitely.

There seemed to be a menagerie ... up the chimney?

Steve stared suspiciously at the old inglenook fireplace. Had his mother hidden a TV up the chimney? She was always playing silly tricks. As he stared, there was a slight fall of soot. Steve was certain he could hear someone chuckle ...

With a jump in his heart, Steve ran and stuck his head up the chimney. It was soot black; he couldn't see a thing. But the owl hooted again – softly, this time, as if in welcome. And then again, the little giggle.

He knew that laugh.

'You!' Quickly Steve ran to the drawer and rummaged about for the torch. He had it and was on his way back to have a proper look when his mother came back in.

'Cheese! Cheese and tomata! 'Am and pickle! Cheese! Egg salad! Cheese! Oh, my God!' she wailed. She dashed about getting things from the fridge. 'There are thousands of 'em,' she exclaimed. 'All swilling beer and sandwiches and practically eating cigarettes – just like the cartoons. I'll have to go into Grassington for more supplies ... You butter the bread, I'll do the fillings .... Oh, God, Steven, you haven't even started. Oh, God. Oh, God ...'

Steve seized the knife and began buttering, while his mother took over the tomatoes.

'I cut mesel',' he said.

'Don't bleed on bread,' she replied.

Frantically slicing tomatoes, his mother fumbled and dropped the knife on the floor. 'Calm down. Calm down,' she told herself. 'They can just bloody wait, that's all.' She picked up her knife and started again, more slowly this time.

Steve glanced behind him to the chimney. Some soot had fallen down onto the shelves below.

'Oh – one o'clock,' said his mother, glancing at the clock on the wall. 'We might as well ...' She leaned across the table and put the radio on.

'This is the World at One ...' said the radio. 'First, the news headlines ...' Steve could have groaned aloud.

It was the same stuff – the Tiger Park. Lila had not been caught, and, unbelievably for such a large and prominent animal, there had been no sightings and no fresh tracks. The two dead men found above Malham Cove had been identified as members of Manchester Triad with links to Hong Kong. Police were directing their enquiries to inner Manchester.

Behind Steve and his mother, there was a fall of soot. Steve glanced back. His mother saw his gaze, followed it.

'Jackdaws are back,' she sighed. 'If I catch 'em, I'll make 'em into sandwiches.'

'Police are also asking for anyone who might know of the whereabouts of a young girl, aged fourteen or fifteen, who they think might be able to help them with their enquiries. "Anyone who knows who this girl might be, or her whereabouts, should contact us immediately," said a police spokesman. "We believe she was present during the attack and that she remains in the area. We're looking for a slight, blonde-haired girl ..."' The policeman gave a description of the strange clothes Steve had given her. '"We should stress," added the police spokesman, "that whilst the girl may be of slight build, and whilst she may be an innocent party, there is also the possibility that she is dangerous. We advise members of the public not to approach her. At this stage, however, we are seeking to eliminate her from our enquiries ..."'

'At last!' exclaimed Steve's mother. She seized a tottering pile of sandwiches, flung them onto plates and dashed back into the pub. Steve could hear her calling ... 'Number 23? 'Am and tomata? Who ordered 'am and tomata?'

Steve grabbed the torch and shone it up the chimney. A couple of yards up was a narrow ledge, and he fully expected to see her there, grinning down at him.

But the chimney was empty. As he watched, some soot fell on his face.

'Hello? Are you there? Hello?' he softly called. There was no answer except another fall of soot, quite heavy this time, on his upturned face.

Steve wiped the soot out of his eyes and ran out of the back door to try and get a look at the chimney. He waited there for minutes but there was no sign. Then his mother was screaming at him to come back and help. Stunned, Steve went back to slice sandwich fillings.

On the radio was a report on Sheila Abbot, whose husband had died defending the tigers. Nicky had become a hero. Sheila paid tribute to his bravery and spoke of her hope for compensation from the management of the Tiger Park. This, however, was unlikely. The Tiger Park was collecting no receipts from the public now it had closed. Of the two recaptured tigers, one, Donna, was dead; while the other, Will, was still critical. Only one cub remained – one of Lila's month-old babies who had miraculously escaped the slaughter and had been found wandering alone in the park earlier that morning.

With no tigers to show the Park was unlikely to get any money in the foreseeable future. Unless someone could be found willing to invest, Malham Tiger Park faced certain closure.

6

Sirrah

Lila kept to the long shadows of the stone walls. It was dark; she dared not travel like this by day as her coat, such perfect camouflage amongst the trees, stood out like a beacon here on the bare fields. Fortunately she had other ways of hiding.

As she approached the place where Sirrah was hidden, she was transformed; she wanted no tiger scent here. She sniffed the ground, the rocks, the tufts of grass, the long fallen-down walls. Even in her other shape she could smell that dogs and men had been here. They had even investigated the opening of the cave into the ground, but had gone no further.

Lila slid through the narrow opening into the ground.

Underground the darkness was total, but she understood the way with her nose and quickly found the place. She began to pull at the heap of rocks. Inside was a low growl; answering, she was again transformed. She pulled with her paws at the remaining rocks until the hole was big enough.

Sirrah lay a few paces from where she had left him. He had crawled across the cave to drink at the stream. He lifted his head slightly and drew back his lips, a welcoming grimace of pain.

Overjoyed that he was still alive, Lila crouched low and licked his muzzle. Sirrah made noises of welcome deep in his throat. He tried to sit up to say hello but his legs would not support him any longer. He collapsed, panting. He was in terrible pain.

Lila had no way of knowing that he had to have medical attention very soon. Left here, he would certainly die. It passed through her mind to get help. She had a friend ... she could fetch him, show him. He might know something she did not, even though he had been unable to save Will or Donna. But Lila did not yet know how much she could trust Steve, or how much she could make him understand.

Besides, she had another mission uppermost in her mind.

When the clouds covered the moon, Lila crept out and took a sheep. She ate half and dragged the rest of the carcass back and laid it near Sirrah. He sniffed at the dead animal and tried a couple of licks, but he soon gave up and rested his head.

Now Lila had to go away for a few days. Sirrah would live ... or he would die. That was the nature of things. He was her mate, the father of her cubs and he meant more to her than anyone else in the world. But even Lila could do nothing about death.

She licked a patch of wool off the flesh and tore the skin with her teeth to encourage him. Then, while the night was still deep she left him, piling the stones in a heap once more over the entrance. Had she known of such things, she would have prayed that he would be better by the time she got back. Instead, sitting on the stones outside, she cried farewell to him. He answered weakly. Then she set off at a fast pace, heading south. She wanted to get as far as she could while the darkness hid her.

7

The Killings

The next day the sightings began.

It was at this time that the fear of the tigress began to spread beyond the Dales into Yorkshire and beyond. The sightings came from all over, from Scotland to Hampshire, from Wales to Norfolk. Lila became a ghost. She was seen in the cities, the Fens, the moors, forests and towns. Every breath in the dark, every half-glimpsed shadow, every fear, every nightmare was the tigress. It was as if Lila had escaped to haunt the land that fed her.

Among the various reports of things that could as well have been big dogs and calves and ponies at night as tigers, were a handful of clear sightings. Over the next couple of days, a pattern began to emerge.

The big cat seemed to have left the Malham area and was heading south. There were sightings of her stalking sheep on the fields under Pendle Hill and again in an old quarry near Ramsbottom. Then again, north of Bolton. A man walking his dog in the late evening heard a rustle in the grass and discovered a slain sheep. The sheep was uneaten; he must have disturbed her at her kill. The man was thought lucky to have escaped with his life.

The following night in a village outside Manchester the theory was confirmed when a small pony was killed in a field. No other animal but a big cat could have done this. The hunt was relaunched with fresh vigour.

Policemen, helicopters and dogs descended on the village and searched the fields near where the pony had been found. There, sure enough, were the pug marks of the tigress. Some droppings were found not far off. They tracked her as far as a stream running under a road bridge just north of the village of Breightmet. There, once again, Lila disappeared.

The panic among the villagers nearby was worse than ever. What sort of beast was it that appeared only to kill, then vanished? The area was put under a curfew, searched from top to bottom. Roadblocks were put up on every little track. But nothing was seen or heard of the tigress. No one had the slightest idea where she would appear again. The general theory was that she was heading for Manchester.

* * *

Michael Sum's father had emigrated to England in the fifties, where he had worked in Manchester's China-town as a waiter in a restaurant. He had been extremely disapproving when his son had become involved with the Triad but Michael had done very well from his line of work. While his father and mother still lived in a small flat in Chinatown, he was already the owner of a fine detached house in a well-off suburb.

Tonight, while his young wife prepared his meal in their luxury kitchen, Michael was in a sitting room on the first floor leafing through a number of proposals and options his accountant had prepared for him. He was planning a trip to Hong Kong. The recent operation in Malham, among others, had paid well. He had enough money now to invest and become the respectable businessman his father wanted.

Michael yawned and leaned back in his chair. The proposals bored him. He would probably invest some of the money anyway, just to keep his father happy. But he had no desire to leave the Triad. Why should he? He was good at it.

Michael sniffed the smells of the good food coming up from the kitchen. He got up and pressed a button on the intercom to complain to his wife that he was up here working and starving half to death while she played about downstairs.

'The cook can't cook the food faster than the food takes to cook,' his wife told him amiably in Chinese. Michael grinned to himself and wandered across the room. He wasn't really complaining; he just liked to use the intercom.

To the rear of the house was a large, well-cared-for garden with an ancient growth of wistaria climbing up to the balcony. Michael wandered across and opened the French windows to the balcony to look out at the floodlit shrubs and statues. He felt very good indeed about what he owned. He stood gazing over his property in this manner when a noise below him made him look down. There, standing on the lawn by the foot of the wistaria, gazing blandly up at him, was a tiger.

Michael yelped. He slammed the French windows shut and ran across the room. On the way his shin cracked against the heavy glass coffee table with the proposals on and he tripped over, landing with a thud on his side. Cursing and hobbling, he flung himself at the door and wrenched it open.

The whole process took Michael about five seconds. In that time the tigress launched herself up the wistaria and clawed up to the balcony, leaving two-inch deep claw marks in the hard trunk; then leaped straight through the glass doors and across the room in a cascade of shattered glass. Had he continued in his flight, Michael would have managed one more step towards the stairs but he half turned at the sound of the glass shattering. The tigress knocked him down and landed with both feet on his chest, crushing his ribs, heart and lungs in the process. He was already dead as she took his head into her mouth and crushed his skull.

By the time his wife got out of the kitchen and up the stairs to investigate the noise the tigress was already back down, over the thick cypress hedge and trotting away in another garden two hundred metres distant from where Michael first saw her a couple of minutes before.

By nine o'clock the following morning, it was apparent that the streets were far more clogged than was normal, even for the Manchester rush hour. It took the authorities a while to understand what was happening.

In the night there had been four deaths in three separate incidents in localities in Manchester, three men and one woman. Someone's girlfriend had been unlucky enough to disturb Lila at her work. Despite numerous assurances over the radio and television that the streets were safe and that the police expected the tiger to be caught and shot very soon indeed, the pale men, women and children sat in their cars, their faces tight and afraid, waiting for the traffic to move them another precious few metres away from the terror. Lila had come: everyone wanted to get out.

In all truth the news was not reassuring. The same news bulletins full of reassuring messages showed the police out searching the streets, armed to the teeth. No one was fooled. All the rules were being broken. The term, Spirit Tiger, was being bandied about. That an ordinary animal could make its way, unseen, into the heart of a great city, enter apartment blocks, kill and then leave, equally unseen? Impossible! For the first time in thousands of years, the people of England found an animal among them that had powers greater than they did.

The dead woman was European, but the men were all Chinese members of the Triad, the same organisation that the two dead men from Malham had come from. The same gang the police suspected of being behind the Malham Park massacre. Lila was continuing her revenge.

By afternoon, with the tigress still on the loose and with no clues at all as to her whereabouts, the police developed a theory of their own. According to this Lila was not on the loose at all. The gang – or a rival gang – had captured her alive. They were driving her in a van from place to place – the field by Pendle Hill, the other locality just outside Bolton – so that the tiger could be sighted. This was just to spread confusion and terror.

The real purpose of the kidnapped tiger was as an implement of murder. She was driven at night to the houses of the chosen victims and set loose on them. It was all to do with some internal Triad feud. The stories being circulated about the supernatural powers of the tiger were just designed to scare the victims – and potential victims – even more.

This theory was picked up by the media and circulated widely. It was grabbed eagerly by a nervous population. This was a rational explanation in a rational world. How could a tiger move unseen through a big city? In a crate inside a van, where no one could see it. It made sense.

The next night the tiger struck again, this time in central Manchester. Two men, one a prominent member of the Triad, the other, his bodyguard, were killed in the penthouse flat of a luxury apartment block overlooking the city centre. This time, the killing actually seemed to reassure people that the police theory was true. Manchester was a major city. It was full of people always on the move. No animal that big could live undetected on its streets. The whole thing was obviously some bizarre, ritualistic Triad feud.

Roadblocks were set up. No van or lorry that moved in the city went unsearched. The police were certain that this time they had the measure of it. They confidently announced that Manchester had seen an end to the killings.

That night, three more men were killed, all in the safety of their own homes, all in different parts of the city. The tiger had chased one of them through the house, destroying three separate heavy pine doors to do it. The terrified victim then fled into the garden, locking the French windows behind him. Neighbours had heard the shattering of glass as the tiger came through after him, followed by the destruction of the garden shed as his final hiding place was annihilated. They rang the police to the sound of the dying man's screams and the tiger's roars.

The police were there within minutes, roadblocks set up to intercept the fleeing gangsters in their van. They tracked the tiger two gardens further down, where her feet left traces of loam on a neighbour's patio. And there the trail ended as mysteriously and suddenly as it always did. No trace of tiger or Triad was ever found. Not a van or lorry in miles was left unsearched.

The next day, after yet another broadcast reassuring the public that everything was well under control, the Chief of Police returned to his office and, behind locked doors, ordered his officers to contact privately any experts on big cat behaviour that they could track down.

'Maybe they'll have some ideas. We don't appear to have any left,' he said.

The only trouble was, the experts were as confused as everyone else.

One thing the police did discover: members of the Triad were leaving the country in droves. The police reckoned that sixteen members had left for Hong Kong and Taiwan. These were the gang's best men. Their going brought about a sudden upsurge in gang warfare in Manchester as rival gangs fought for the business suddenly left unattended. Overnight, this Triad gang had been almost wiped out.

Along with the men so far killed, the number who had left added up to just about the same number estimated to have been present at the Tiger Park the night of the massacre. As suddenly as they had started, the killings came to an end. The police came to the conclusion that whoever – or whatever – was doing them had run out of victims. After a couple of days they had reason to hope that the deaths were over

The police did not take into account Sheila Abbot.

* * *

On a still, misty day in north London the traffic piled up along the big roads. The endless lines of cars growled their way through the mists, which seemed to trap the exhaust fumes and hold them stinking in the air. It was getting worse. Houses just thirty or forty metres away were disappearing from sight.

Four days in London had given Sheila sinusitis. Her sister, with whom she was staying, told her it wasn't usually as bad as this; it was the weather that made it so bad.

'It's the cars that make it so bad,' pointed out Sheila. How could people live in these conditions? The bloody country had too many people and not enough space. She would have killed to get back to Africa. She would have killed to get back to Yorkshire come to that, but she was too scared.

Sheila Abbot walked down the road, her head throbbing. She was looking for a telephone booth, but when she found one she paused nervously outside, scared to take the next step into her nightmare. She started to think of Nicky; wished he was here to help her, but she put the thought quickly out of her head. She couldn't afford to let herself think of Nicky; it made her cry.

There had been a message popped through the front door a couple of days before. From Lee Yung. He wanted her to ring him that evening at seven. She had been instructed to use a public telephone booth, to minimise any risk that the call might be traced.

She had rung, but from her sister's phone at home, trying to tape the call. Of course the number did not go directly to Lee. She had reached someone else, who very quickly knew what was going on. The phone went dead almost immediately.

That night a very polite young man rang her bell and advised her nicely to do as she was told. Now, she was doing as she had been told.

The phone was answered immediately. There was a pause – a few clicks, doubtless as tests were run. Then, the soft but enthusiastic voice of Mr Lee.

'Good evening, Mrs Abbot. We thought you were deserting us.'

Sheila got straight to the point. 'When am I going to get my money?'

'Of course, you realise that not all the goods were delivered ...'

'We agreed what would happen in that event. You knew the risks. I was supposed to get paid immediately on delivery.'

'And, of course, the main item is still at large.'

'There's nothing I can do about that.'

'No?'

'Mr Lee. I've lost my husband. I've lost my job.' She took a deep breath. 'Can I ask you this once to be square with me?'

'I am as square as ...' Mr Lee giggled. '... as a football pitch, Mrs Abbot. What makes you think I am not square?'

'Am I on the list?'

'List, Mrs Abbot?'

Sheila Abbot tried to control herself. 'Do you plan on taking my life?'

Lee sounded puzzled. 'What for?'

'I'm not a fool, Mr Lee. Not that much of a fool, anyway. Someone shot my husband. Now it seems that the other men involved in the raid are getting killed at the rate of two or three a day, by a tiger. Unlike some of your colleagues I do not have the money to flee the country, unless you choose to pay me. It would be easier and cheaper all round simply to kill me, I suppose ...'

She tried to keep her voice still, but she was shaking with fear. Nicky had been right; this was out of her league altogether.

Lee laughed. 'Your corpse is of no value to anyone. Why should I waste valuable resources on such an unpromising investment? I promise you, Mrs Abbot, you are of no interest to me or to the Triad. As for the other deaths, I am on good terms with these organisations and I have no wish to spoil a good relationship by killing their people.'

'Except a small matter of a quarter of a million pounds or so which you owe me.'

'If I choose not to pay you, Mrs Abbot, I shall simply not pay you. No need for such extremes as murder.'

Sheila did not believe him, but there was no point in arguing the case. 'If you're not killing those men, who is?'

'The tigress, of course. Lila. She is taking her revenge.'

Sheila bit her lip. All such nonsense ... The man was clearly playing games with her! Apart from anything, she was certain that Lee himself was someone – someone very high up – in the organisation of the Manchester Triads.

'Just ... tell me what you want.'

'You don't believe me? Of course it is unlikely. How can the tigress get through the crowded streets of such a large city, unnoticed? How can she enter the apartments of these armed and dangerous men? How can she kill and then leave, unseen? These same questions are interesting the police very much. But I promise you the police are on the wrong track. Lila is young, but she is a very powerful spirit. It is her you have to fear, Mrs Abbot – not me. But to get to the point. You will at least understand something now of how I feel. My illness has progressed since we last saw each other. A matter of life and death, Mrs Abbot – to me, as well as you. I need this medicine very soon if I am not to die. It is in both our interests to kill Lila.'

'I don't see how I can help you with all this any more.'

'But I insist. I am happy to pay you for your services so far. I have another proposition to put to you.'

'I don't want to be involved in this any further. This isn't poaching, it's murder.'

'I suggest we meet. I will give you your money and you, as a favour to me, will oblige me by at least listening.'

'I can listen, I suppose.'

'That's all I ask. Of course this is not a matter where we can really hand over a cheque. Cash is the way we do business, Mrs Abbot. As it happens I have some business myself, in Malham. I suppose you will be attending your husband's memorial service on Sunday there?'

'I ... haven't made up my mind.'

'It would be very suspicious if you were to miss it. I will be staying in Grassington that weekend. I shall book us both rooms. The same hotel will be convenient. We shall find the opportunity to do our business over the weekend, I'm sure.'

'But ...'

'I will stick to the agreed payment per tiger delivered. That is a quarter of a million pounds so far, as you say.'

'Yes ...'

'Don't sound so disbelieving, Mrs Abbot. It is not good business to make an arrangement and then break it. I would make my life very hard if I were to do that. I have no need to be greedy these days. See you on Saturday, Mrs Abbot.'

Mr Lee put down the telephone and leaned his head back in his seat. He was exhausted. The cancer inside him had eaten him away until he was no more than skin and bones. He looked tinier than ever. But he was pleased with his work.

Sheila would be there; he could be sure of that. He had no intention of cheating her, or killing her. That was

97

not why he wanted her in Malham. Sheila Abbot and himself were the only two people left alive in the country who had been involved in the massacre at Malham Tiger Park. He would gladly have used himself for bait. It was possible, perhaps, that Lila would know he shared the guilt. She had many gifts. Maybe, maybe not. But she would certainly know all about Sheila, who had actually been there ...

Mr Lee had every confidence that if Sheila Abbot returned to Malham, Lila would not be far behind her.

8

Lila

There had been a succession of a hot spring days – a fierce sun that cut through the cool spring air and burned you quickly, if you didn't keep covered up. The heat was well suited to the arrival of the wild tiger. Steve had been earning some money by getting the pub garden into order – creosoting the swings and climbing frame, weeding the flowerbeds, cutting the grass. He got himself sunburned doing it.

Things had calmed down only somewhat since the tigress left the area. People were still being advised to stay close to the village until she was caught. Some believed she had never left the area at all, that the killings in Manchester were a separate affair and that Lila lay hidden in the high valleys. But the media had all disappeared, a few of the braver hill walkers and potholers had come back, the farmers rode about on their tractors and Range Rovers without their shotguns. Steve was still scared to go on his own into the hills, although he would have loved to catch a glimpse of the tiger.

Today, a Saturday, the wind had turned, bringing a mass of cloud from the north-east and a cold wind. Suddenly the hot weather was gone and in its place there was sleet flung against the narrow windowpanes of The World Around. People drove or huddled their anoraks under their chins if they had to go out on foot.

Inside the pub a huge log fire was blazing and in the corridor, rows of anoraks and steaming socks from wet hill walkers dripped on the stone flags. Mrs Hattersly was doing a roaring trade in home-made steak and kidney pie.

Steve was at a loose end. He'd read a book. There was nothing on TV, his best friends were busy. He'd tried building an Aerofix model left over from his birthday, but he didn't really like the things. His fingers always got hopelessly sticky.

He left his room, chewing the film of dried glue off his fingers, and went down a flight of stairs to lean on the wide, deep sill. The window looked out from the side of the house, down past the village to the hills, grey with sleet.

The pain about the massacre of the tigers was down to a dull ache that never left him. He had been thrilled to live next to one of the biggest populations of tigers left anywhere in the world. Now, their bones were being ground down in the vain hope of curing some old man's rheumatism.

The sleet dribbled down the windowpane, hurried through the air.

Was Lila out there? And Sirrah?

It was generally accepted now that Sirrah was dead, recaptured on the night of the massacre by the fleeing gangsters. But Lila was still alive – for the time being. Mike Craven had been on television stressing the importance of her recapture. Will had recovered from his bullet wounds, one of Lila's cubs had survived the slaughter. Together they might form the basis of a new breeding colony of Siberian tigers. World wide, only around a hundred of these animals remained, scattered throughout zoos all over the world. Malham Tiger Park had been the only colony still hunting for prey. It was a terrible loss, but they had to do what they could to get going again.

Steve sighed and peered out through the grey air, as if he could catch a glimpse of pale, fierce orange ...

From somewhere upstairs, his mother called, 'Steven! Steven!'

Steve looked behind him in surprise. Her voice was coming from the rooms at the top of the flight of stairs. How on earth had she got up there without him seeing her?

'Steven! Steven!'

'What?'

'Steven!'

'What do you want?'

'Steven! Steven!'

Steve tutted and walked up towards her. Why didn't she just tell him what she wanted instead of sitting there going, 'Steven, Steven, Steven,' all the time, like a parrot?

The voice called again as he walked past his room. What was she doing in there? She must have sneaked past him when he was standing on the stairs.

He pushed the door roughly open. 'What are you going on about ...?' he began. Then he froze. It wasn't his mother at all ...

She was sitting cross-legged on his table, on top of his books and pens. She'd got rid of the clothes he'd given her and was wearing black leggings, sneakers and a grey cotton sweatshirt. She grinned.

'Steven! Steven!' she mimicked. She put her hand to her mouth and laughed quietly at his dumbfounded face. Then she called like a wolf and hooted like an owl.

Steve began to grin. She was brilliant! 'You fooled me! But can you talk now?' he added hopefully.

The girl lay down on the table and stared at him, smiling. 'Steven,' she said again, in his mother's voice. It was perfect. She was a wonderful mimic. But she couldn't speak a word.

Steve closed the door behind him. He was becoming scared now. This girl was wanted by the police. He ought to ...

'What do you want?' he asked impatiently. The girl, sprawled on her side on his table top, propped up on one elbow, looked at him lazily through half-closed eyes.

'What do you want?' he repeated.

She must have got something of his intention, for now she propped herself up on one elbow and held her hand out to him in a pleading gesture, as she had that very first time. Then, she stretched her hand towards him and then placed it over her heart. Her face twisted with distress.

Then, she lay back down on the table and regarded him with the same sleepy eyes, all expression gone.

Was she teasing him? She seemed to be going through these gestures as if she had only just learnt them.

Steve said, 'Where have you been?' He still didn't know how much she understood. 'The police are looking for you, did you know? You'll have to give yourself up.'

The girl half turned her head to gaze out of the window.

'What happened that night? You were with them, weren't you?' He waited, sucking his teeth nervously, thinking. He didn't even know whose side she was on! Just because she'd made friends with him didn't mean anything. She might be playing games with him.

'We have to get those men that killed the tigers – you could help. Unless ... Did you help them? Were you – are you one of them?' Again, no answer. She was studying her forearm now. She licked it thoughtfully.

'The gang quarrelled, that's it, isn't it? What about those tigers ...?' Now she looked up and stared at him, stared so hard he felt like a rabbit in the long gaze of her eyes. 'Were they ... did you know they were in the barn? Were you ...' He hesitated, it seemed so unreal. '... hiding them?' Her gaze remained silent, intent. 'Then who were you waiting for?'

The girl wiped her eye with the back of her hand and looked away. She yawned widely, and sighed.

'Why can't you talk?' begged Steve angrily. 'Or won't you?'

He looked at her eyes. Around the small dark oval pupil, they were amber. There were no whites.

Her eyes were inhuman.

Steve began to babble. 'What about the other tiger – she killed those two men. A man-eater, they're calling her. What about ...?' He cleared his throat, unwilling to say the word. 'What about ... Lila? Lila?'

At the sound of her name the girl turned to face him, her amber eyes suddenly hot with fury and grief. Steve felt a distant roaring deep inside. He wanted to turn and flee the room, but he was suddenly unable to move. His muscles were locked in a grip not his own. The roaring got louder and louder, closer and closer. It began to form a shape that he dreaded to understand. She was speaking to him – not with her voice or with her mind but with her soul. Into his heart she poured what she wanted to say. The room seemed to shake; he became convulsed with fear as the roaring formed into some shape he understood.

'I AM THE TIGER,' it said. 'I AM THE TIGER.'

Steve sank to his hands and knees and the noise vanished. He had been plucked suddenly out of a screaming whirlpool. He stood up. The girl was sitting up staring curiously at him, as if to see if this latest trick had worked.

His imagination, surely ... Surely ...

He looked at the girl, her amber eyes watching, waiting. She got to her knees again and held out her hands once more in supplication.

No. It was nonsense – no. Even though she had eyes like no eyes he had ever seen, even though ...

Because if she was ...

'What about those men? The men above the cove and in Manchester? Have you ... been there? Listen ... listen ...' He had to say something, in case the roaring came back ... had to come up with some idea to explain all this away.

'You're on the side of the tigers, aren't you?' She didn't nod, she just looked at him. She didn't even seem confused. She lay down on her front, propped up on her forearms, folded her hands in front of her, and waited.

'The people at the Tiger Park – Mike Craven – you know Mike?' She had lifted her head and regarded him closely. 'Mike Craven?' said Steve again. He was definitely getting through. Was that a nod? 'We should go to see him – he'll be fair.' Steve babbled on, trying to get somewhere, he had no idea where. 'The people at the Tiger Park are good people, you know that. They'll help. I'm just a boy, but they ... What about Nicky Abbot? You know, do you? Yes, he lost his life protecting the tigers ... he was a brave man, a hero.'

He was certainly getting somewhere, but he was not sure he liked what was happening. The girl was fascinated, but the look on her face was furious. She was on her knees and fingertips, now, her face coming closer and closer towards him as she crouched lower. And at the back of his mind, the roaring began again. More words. But Steve was scared of her words. He babbled on, talking louder and louder in an effort to shut off whatever she was doing to him.

'Someone shot him ... one of the poachers shot him. Yes. They're burying him tomorrow, his wife's here ...' He was almost shouting now. 'Do you know her? She worked there too, you must have seen her ...? Sheila. She's in Grassington. She ...'

As he spoke, the roaring grew and Steve was yelling to try and drown it out. The girl was leaning so far forward that her nose was almost touching his. Steve backed off, screaming in fear, trying to close off his mind to the words he could feel budding inside him.

The girl swelled. She literally grew before his eyes. Her eyes glittered desperately. In a fit of rage and frustration she flung herself off the table and swung with both fists at the wardrobe standing in a corner.

The wardrobe shattered. It was heavy oak but her fists went straight through as if it was paper. Then she seized it by the sides and flung it across the room like a cardboard box. It crashed and broke. Her form seemed to be melting with rage. She was changing ...

'Stop – please stop ...' begged Steve. She turned to glare at him ... and then from downstairs there was an exclamation at the thunderous noise. The next second he heard his mother rushing upstairs to see what was going on.

'Steven!'

'Steven!' The girl repeated it scornfully, in exactly his mother's voice. The bedroom door was flung open. His mother began, 'What...' But she got no further. There was the girl crouched on all fours like a cat about to spring amid the remains of the shattered wardrobe and scattered clothes. The girl began to scream at her. As she screamed she changed. Her form began to flicker, her voice warbled between the high scream of the young girl and the tiger's roar – from thunder to scream and back to thunder. But it ended on a full roar and there was Lila the killer ready to spring, her lips drawn back in rage, trapped in the tiny room, Steve's mother standing before the only means of escape ...

'No! Lila!' Steve flung himself forward. He seized

her helplessly by the neck – as if he could stop this! He buried his face in the thick fur. 'No, Lila, no, no ...' He heard his mother gasp and knew she had sunk to her knees and hung her head, waiting for death.

'My mother, Lila – no – no! She wasn't there! Leave her! Leave her!'

He clung to her. He felt under the fur and skin her inexorable muscle. She was rigid with rage and fear. There was a long moment. Then, the door closed.

He looked up. His mother was gone.

The tiger's head was inches from his own. 'Lila,' he said. He stroked her fierce head, trying to calm her. She was the spirit after all, pure magic in this age of machines. But for all her strength, she was terribly alone. Full of fear and pity, Steve seized her fierce head and hugged her, hugged her, hugged her hard. He felt her relax and soften.

And it was the girl again. She lay in his arms. She clung to him, buried her head into his collar bones and began to sob and sob and sob.

'Steven,' she wept. 'Steven. Steven.'

Her face was wet with tears. Steve began to weep too. He held her tightly, hugged her and loved her with all his heart, as if love could make it all right.

'I'm sorry, Lila, I'm so sorry, I'm so sorry ...'

The two lay there like this for five full minutes. When the tears died away he touched her hair and her shoulders, closely watched her small, wide-eyed face. Lila touched his wet cheeks. 'Steven,' she said, curiously watching him. It was a miracle. As a tiger she was wonderful but unreachable, unknowable.

He wanted her to stay as a girl forever.

It was a thought that broke the spell. Steve suddenly remembered his mother.

He stood up hurriedly. 'I must see her – see what she does ...' he explained. Lila stared at him blankly.

'Wait here,' he commanded. He ran down the stairs. Where had she gone? He called, no answer. He ran round the house and heard the comfortable babble of voices from the pub. Hadn't she warned them that the tiger was in the house? He ran into the pub. Everything was so ... normal. He ran on into the kitchen and there she was, calmly spooning mashed potatoes onto three warm plates.

'What on earth was that noise, Steven?' she asked him crossly. 'It sounded like you had a rhinoceros up there.'

'No ...' he began. He looked curiously into her face. 'Don't you remember?' he asked.

'I remember ceiling nearly coming through. What were it?'

'I was ... I was trying to get the Monopoly from top o' the wardrobe and it ... fell on me.'

'Oh, my God ...! Dear – are you all right?'

'I am. But wardrobe's broken, I'm sorry.'

'Can't be, it's built like a battleship! Oh well, we can get it fixed, I suppose.'

'I don't think so, it's very badly broken ...' said Steve, thinking of the mass of splinters.

'Help me serve this out, darling, there's a dear,' said his mother, cashing in on his guilty look.

'Just a minute...' Steve ran out of the kitchen. He heard her calling crossly behind him, but he just charged on. How could he miss what was waiting for him? But upstairs, the window was half open. Of Lila, there was no sign.

He put out his head and called her name, softly. But she had left him again.

9

Sheila

'Fear in Malham tonight, as the man-eater returns to the Yorkshire Dales,' said the newsreader gravely.

Sheila Abbot, in her hotel room at Grassington, pulled a face. Not that she gave any credence to those stories about the escaped tigress hunting down those involved in the massacre – she was too hard-headed for that – but it gave her the creeps all the same. She knew the police theory was wrong. Lila had not been captured. She was at large all right. Now they had found fresh pug marks at Malham. A bullock was found dead and partly eaten only a few miles away. The tiger was haunting the village once more.

The big cats. You had to admire them. She was always clever, Lila. You couldn't help wondering how on earth she had evaded capture for so long.

Sheila's own theory was, the tiger had never left the Dales. Why should she? It was her ground, so to speak. The killing must have been done by men and disguised so as to make it appear that Lila was doing the dirty work. What else could it be? Doubtless some Triad rivalry had been going on. The killers had taken advantage of the escaped tiger to spread fear and cover their tracks – successfully, too. They had the police turning cartwheels.

There had been Chinese people on the TV. Spirit Tiger, they called her. Just another way of spreading fear. No. The gang who took part in the massacre was being punished not for their success at killing, but for their failure to kill enough.

She had been a member of that gang; she had been a part of that failure ...

The news continued.

'Friends and relatives gathered in Malham tonight for the funeral tomorrow of Nicky Abbot, the murdered Tiger Park guide, who lost his life in an effort to save the tigers. David Bury reports ...'

Tears sprang suddenly to Sheila's eyes. The worst of it was, he hadn't wanted to do this job. He'd only been going along with her; he disagreed with it, really. She had always been the businesswoman; he had always done as she told him. But in the end he had been right.

It was too late now.

There was a tribute from Mike Craven – as usual, trying to sell his precious Tiger Park. What was left of it.

'Nicky gave his life trying to save the tigers. If we can capture Lila alive there will at least be a breeding pair as a nucleus to re-start the colony,' said the Park Director on the TV. And there was Sheila herself. She stared in fascination as her TV image spoke to her with her own words, as she sat on the edge of the bed in her hotel room.

'He was a dear man ... friends and relations across the world have sent messages. I just want to get it over with ...'

'Is it true,' asked the interviewer, 'that you're hoping for some sort of compensation from the Tiger Park?'

Sheila saw herself stiffen on the screen. 'I have to live somehow,' she said shortly.

'But you know that the Tiger Park is on the verge of bankruptcy? The Park has said that you could force them to close. Do you think that's what your husband would have wanted?'

'My husband was a brave man who gave everything for the tigers. I think I can be allowed to have some sort of living now that he's dead,' she said curtly. Her face had gone hard. How ugly she looked when she went like that. She hated those bloody reporters!

'I'd like just to remember him as he was ...'.

In her hotel room, Sheila wiped the tears out of her eyes. Damn it, if she had the money she was owed she'd happily let the Park off the hook, but she hadn't a bean to her name. What was she supposed to do? The tigers were doomed anyway. It was as Lee had said – their time was over. Well, if he paid her – *if* he paid her – she wouldn't press for compensation. There was no need to be greedy, after all.

Sheila got up to make herself a cup of tea from the kettle on the cupboard. There was a tray with teabags, coffee, chocolate and so on. She would have liked to go out for a walk really, but at nine, in one hour, she was supposed to go to room 5 to meet Mr Lee. She had not exactly been told not to go out but there were bodyguards walking past her door every few minutes. For her own protection, she had been told. They were very discreet. No one else would have guessed why they were there.

Sheila bowed her head and bit her lip. She was

terrified. By doing business with Lee Yung she had become his creature. At best it would be blackmail of some sort, she had decided. The chances of getting paid were very slim. At worst, it would be her life.

There was, however, one thing she could do. Sheila was not going to give up without a struggle. In her handbag was a letter, a copy of which she had left with her lawyer, to be opened and read in the event of her sudden death. In the letter she gave details of the whole plan of the raid on the Tiger Park and its execution – her involvement, her husband's, the Triad men – and of course, everything she had on the mysterious Mr Lee, including a rather good pencil sketch.

Well, it was probably a waste of time. No doubt the police had known about Lee Yung for years. It was a question of getting the evidence, and a dead witness was as good as no witness. But it was the only card she had, and if there were to be any threat to her, she would play it.

Sheila went to the window. It was twilight. Her room looked out onto the car park at the back of the hotel. Lee had got her one of the cheaper rooms, another way of showing her that she was not worth much any more.

On the tarmac below, a young girl paused and stared intently at the first floor window. Her amber eyes fixed on the figure moving behind the curtains. As she watched, a large man in a smart suit walked slowly across from a car towards the building. He had done this every ten minutes for the past two hours. The girl walked round the corner towards the road, then hid and peeked back.

As the man disappeared into the back door, the girl slid out again, keeping close to the wall until she was directly under the window on the left. The wall was plain and unadorned. She reached up and placed her hands against the brickwork.

Inside, Sheila glanced at her watch. Half past eight. Half an hour to go. It was impossible to bear the waiting! Why had he made her come all this way? He could have arranged to pay her off – or polish her off – anywhere.

A proposition, he said. Whatever he wanted, she had to go along with it, she knew that. All she could do was hope she would get her reward and her liberty in the end.

She walked a couple of times around the room. This was no good, she was getting herself worked up. She decided to have a shower. She might as well go to the meeting looking fresh, even if she didn't feel it.

She stripped, stepped into the shower and turned it on. She waited while it heated up, then opened a pack of shower gel with her teeth and began to soap herself.

It was a good shower – the water hissed strongly against her skin. She felt better already. She stood under there for a long time, letting the water wash the apple-scented suds off her skin. She felt better for it. She reached out to turn the shower off and as she did so, heard a slight noise inside her room.

Sheila froze.

The door to her room was locked. The shower was strong but she would have heard it open – wouldn't she?

Quickly she pulled a bathrobe on, got out of the bath and stood by the door, dripping water onto the tiles and listening.

Nothing.

'Who's there? Who is it?'

Nothing. Had she imagined it? Sheila stood still, listening for a full minute. As she stood, trying to breathe quietly, a strange odour crept through the door and filled her nostrils. It took her a while to place it. She was familiar with that smell. She knew it from work ...

It smelt as if a tiger had sprayed on the other side of the door.

Sheila began to pant slightly. She put the bolt on the bathroom door as quietly and quickly as she could and bent her ear close to the door, listening.

She heard the springs of the bed sigh softly, as if someone was gently sitting down on it.

'Who is it?' she begged.

A friendly voice answered. 'Sheila? Sheila?'

Sheila's face twisted. She lifted her knuckles, white with the pressure of her clenched fists, to her mouth. It was horribly cruel. She knew that voice only too well. It was the voice of her dead husband.

'Please ... don't ...' She couldn't cope with this, she couldn't cope. Why this torture?

'I have a letter ...' she stammered. 'You can see it – a copy of it's in my bag. The other is at my lawyer's. If I die, it tells everything about Mr Lee.' She listened again. There was nothing. 'Look in my bag. Tell Mr Lee. Please, just tell him, will you? Please ...'

'Sheila?' said Nicky's voice. He sounded surprised

and a little concerned for her. There was a pause; then, a heavy creak from the floorboards. Sheila knew that some presence was approaching the door to the bathroom. She backed off into a corner by the toilet.

Something very big began to sniff at the crack under the door to the shower.

'Sheila?' said the voice again.

Sheila began to sob. She sank down onto the floor by the toilet. She was now so terrified – and this was a deliberate ploy by her assassin – that she was utterly unable to defend herself even had she the means to do it. She was ready to die.

The door to the bathroom creaked. She watched the screws in the hinges tear slowly out of the wood. Then, the door exploded. It flew across the room and struck her with such violence that it broke her back before she even saw the orange and black horror that had come for her.

'Quick – knock it down. Now, you do as I say!'

The bodyguard glanced at the small crowd that had gathered in the corridor. Inside the room, after the sudden crashing and crushing of wood, there was silence. Then, the growl of a big cat.

The small crowd turned, screaming, and fled, tripping and falling and getting stuck against one another in the corridor. The bodyguard twitched; his legs wanted to go with them. But Mr Lee was even more frightening than the tiger. The man took a number of steps back and glanced at his employer.

'Now,' ordered Mr Lee. The bodyguard grunted and

flung his weight at the door. At the third blow, the door gave and he stumbled in.

The girl was standing at the bedroom window.

'Shoot her,' ordered Mr Lee.

'Boss – it's a girl – I can't ...'

'Shoot her, you fool, she's no girl ...'

'It'll be murder!'

The girl was making little darting runs in front of the window. More people had appeared in the corridor. The guard was terrified of shooting someone in front of witnesses.

'You idiot ... She'll return to what she is when she dies – quick...' Lee Yung cursed the man and made a grab for his gun. Stupid! He should have carried one himself, this of all nights. At the same second the girl pointed towards the bathroom and screamed, 'Tiger! Tiger!'

Both Lee and the bodyguard jumped back and the girl made a run for it. She brushed past the big man and he went flying across the room like a rabbit. Lee was swept aside. As he tumbled to the ground he grabbed ridiculously at his head – too late. The coal black wig that he wore to conceal his bald head – the effects of chemotherapy for his cancer – slipped off. The girl saw it and found time to laugh at him. Then she was off, running, running as fast as a ...

'Shoot her!' howled Lee. He half ran, half crawled across and seized the gun off the idiot bodyguard. He would have the bodyguard killed. His desire for the tigress, which he regarded almost as his own life stolen from him, was so great that his weakness and old age seemed to fall from him. Lila was already round the corner. Lee gave chase. Behind him he heard his other men follow. Cowards! They dared let him go into danger first!

He saw her ahead and lifted the gun, but there were people in the corridor. Despite himself, he let the moment slip for fear of hitting them. Now the girl was down the stairs. He ran after her, jumping down and half falling, clutching the bannister, getting down as fast as his old legs would carry him. He reached the ground floor and followed her through the doorway at the back of the building – and into the night.

It was still and dark. Lee was gasping for breath, but his head was crystal clear. He was in the car park behind the hotel. There was nothing to be seen, only the cars, orange-grey in the light of sodium street lamps. Behind him, his men gathered.

'Lila! I am here. Lila!' He looked around. There was no movement. 'Listen! It was me, Lila. I was the one. I wasn't there, but I arranged everything. It was me. I am your enemy. Will you let me live?'

But then a car swung round the corner and suddenly, in the blaze of its headlamps, he saw the tigress staring at him. He lifted his hand – too late. She had him in her eye.

Lee felt his arm sink down as she took his spirit into hers. Now he needed his men more than ever. They were all around him, he had warned them of this. But would they follow their orders?

One of them raised his gun. Lila saw; she fled as the gunshot blasted through the night and silenced the

118

screams and shouts still coming from inside the hotel. There was a glimpse of the tiger bounding between the parked cars and over the stone wall around the car park. A couple more men fired shots, but too late. There were more screams as people saw the terrible form running like something from a dream through the streets of their town, but Lila had no interest in any of them. A second later she was into the fields and gone.

Lee sighed in relief. Of course his men had been about him, but – what more dangerous game was there to play? He patted his bald head irritably. She had humiliated him by exposing his vanity and his weakness. The whole thing was becoming more personal. Lee had begun to hate the tigress.

A sudden exhaustion overcame him. Under his neat suit, Mr Lee was a bag of skin and bones. Such exercise could kill him. He sagged backwards. One of his men tucked a hand under his arm – discreetly, so that no one would see that the Triad leader was unable to stand alone.

Once again the tigress had escaped him. But she would come back. He had made sure of that. He would let her know where he was. She would come, and then he would have her.

From now on, he must make sure he was always in the presence of armed guards. He must never be on his own again till Lila was dead.

Mr Lee turned to his men. 'Search Mrs Abbot's room. Take anything that relates to me. Quick, the police will be here in minutes ...'

'It's already been done,' one of them said. He broke

off. Somewhere in the hills above, Lila was roaring down at the town.

Later that night, there was a burglary at the Manchester offices of Sorbright and Klee, Solicitors. The safe was emptied. Among the missing documents was the last will and testament of Sheila Abbot and a letter she had requested be opened in the event of her death. No one ever found out what was in it.

10

Calling

Before, it had been clear enough – claw marks on the bodies, the pug marks in blood on the floors of the rooms. But you could always say it was faked because no one had ever seen the culprit. But when Sheila Abbot died in her hotel room in Grassington, it seemed that half the town had seen or heard the tiger roaring and snarling in the bedroom, dashing with all the power and grace of her kind between the cars, running along the pavements and swerving off across the fields. Literally hundreds had heard her roaring in the hills above the town.

And yet, despite all the evidence, no one quite believed it. Your eyes could tell you, your ears could agree. All the evidence could point to it. But no tiger that ever lived could find its way to a locked hotel room and then out to the car park with no one seeing her. It was impossible. Lila was more nightmare than cat.

The investigation went on. The police found Lila's pug marks on the field where so many witnesses said she left the road. The ground was soft, the tracks were clear. They led up the hill and on to a dirt track by an old barn a few hundred metres away, where all trace of the tiger vanished. Dogs and men by the hundred combed the area. They found nothing.

Now, nowhere was safe. What was the point of locking yourself in your room when the tiger could appear like magic where it wanted – on the carpet in the living room, in your bathroom? The police had no idea where to turn next. Half the gangsters had fled the country, even those who had nothing to do with the Tiger Park job. The remainder when questioned, said, 'Spirit Tiger.' The police snorted with contempt at such an answer and continued getting nowhere.

Many people, particularly those with children, began to leave the area to stay with friends and relations until the danger was over. Everything was coming closer and closer to home. Who knew when it would be one of the local children found staring sightlessly at the ceiling in their own sitting room, in a pool of blood?

The locals left; in their place came the media in greater numbers than ever. The day after the killing of Sheila Abbot every room in Malham and the surrounding villages was full with television crews and journalists from all over the world – Japan to Canada, Sri Lanka, Europe, India, Russia, the USA – they all wanted to be part of solving the mystery of the Spirit Tiger in the English Dales.

Only two people knew the truth. One was Mr Lee. The other, Steve.

Lila had taken Steve's spirit into her own as surely as if she had trapped him with her eye. She was haunting him, entering his dreams, filling his mind every waking moment. He wondered if this was some new magic of hers. Her faces – both that of the girl and that of the tiger – were held so vividly in his memory that he could sit and study them, the detail of her eyebrows and of her deep amber-green eyes, as if they were before him in life.

It was no magic. It was friendship, it was fascination, it was love, it was a deep involvement with her fate. Wonderful though she was, Lila could surely not stay free forever. Soon, perhaps, they would find her and kill her.

Steve wanted above all else to rescue her, and he knew how, too. He wanted her to come back and live with him as a girl. She had to relinquish her true shape and nature forever, just in order to live. Just to be with him. 'Be a girl,' he whispered to the darkness as he lay in bed. 'Be a girl. Be a girl ...'

He called to her softly when he entered his room, in the hope that she was hiding nearby. He looked for her in the barn, in the pub, in the streets. He shone the torch up the chimney. But she was never there. His mother noticed how listless and quiet he had become, and was worried. She thought that Steve, like so many of the other local children, was terrorised by the thought of the tiger roaming the hills.

The fact was, his mother was more scared than he was. If the pub hadn't been raking in money she would have cleared the whole family out. All around her the other parents were taking good care of their children, sending them to stay with friends and relations in less dangerous places. In the end she decided that her son had had enough.

'Steven, the police are advising evacuation. Practically everyone else has gone. Your dad and I think you ought to go and stay with Aunt Jenny.'

'What? Go away now?'

'Place is turning into an 'orror movie, it'd be a pity to miss the end,' sympathised his mother. 'But this is real life. You're going to have to go. Things are getting a bit desperate, don't you think?'

'But I want to stay,' begged Steve. 'It's just media madness,' he said, repeating what he'd heard his mother herself say.

'Oh, you reckon journalists killed Sheila Abbot and those men to make a story? People are getting killed, Steven. The whole thing gives me the creeps. I'd go myself but...'

'What? You're staying here and I've got to go?'

'Pub's making a fortune – those journalists drink all the time. Some of them are drunk every lunchtime.'

'Like Dad.'

'I'm not sure success suits him,' said his mother grimly.

'I'll be in a great state if you two get eaten by Lila, won't I? Or Dad dies of drink. An orphan ...' pointed out Steve.

'Oh, don't be daft,' she said, a little too lightly.

'If it's nowt to worry, why're you sending me off?'

'I'm worried about yer ...'

Steve began to panic. She'd made up her mind and there would be no shifting her. He was going to miss the most wonderful thing that had ever happened to him.

'It's not me you're bothered about at all ...' Steve's voice was beginning to wobble. There was no way he could explain how important this was to him – and perhaps to the tigress herself. The tears in his voice only convinced his mother all the more, and he knew it. It was already all arranged. He was to go the very next day to stay with Jenny.

Steve ran out to the pub to try and speak to his dad, but when he got to the bar it was full of strangers. He crashed in with a bang, stared around him at the startled journalists, and ran straight back out into the road.

'What's the matter with the boy?' asked a newspaper-man, leaning with one arm on the bar.

'Oh, I dunno. Upset by all this business, most like,' said Mr Hattersly lightly. He liked to keep family affairs out of the pub whenever possible. He saw the journalist looking thoughtfully after Steve, and cursed to himself. The wretched man'd be chasing his boy down the road in the hope of getting a story next thing. Tears were just another few column inches to these blokes.

He turned back to continue serving. At the back of the bar was a television set. He glanced at his watch. Seven o'clock.

'Eh ... turn on Channel Four, will yer?' he shouted to the folk at that end of the bar. ''Ave a look at the news. See what's been going on in Malham today, shall we?' he joked.

Someone turned over and turned the sound up so the publican could hear. There was a picture of Mike Craven walking in the hills with a small, delicate-looking Chinese man.

'A possible way out for Malham Tiger Park tonight, as the Park Director holds talks with Hong Kong businessman Lee Yung ...' said the newsreader.

'So our Mike's found a buyer for the Park, 'as he? A Chinese, 'n'all. Half of 'em want to grind their bones to

125

make their bread, the other half want to keep 'em as pets,' observed Mr Hattersly. 'Eh, what d'yer reckon?' he asked one of the journalists at the bar. 'Maybe Mr Lee Yung wants to turn Malham Tiger Park into a Soup Farm – what d'yer think?'

The streets were full of strange faces. Malham had always been a tourist town, but there were always people you knew out and about. Now, the locals had disappeared, hiding in their homes or gone away. Instead there were strangers – poking, asking questions, filming. They had completely taken the place over. The babble of nations filled the air.

As Steve left the pub there was a television crew filming the streets. He could see them looking curiously at him. Any minute now they'd come over and start off again, all you had to do was stick your head out of the door and there they were. Just a few words, how do you feel, are you frightened, what do you think about the Tiger Park ...?

Sometimes he thought that the villagers were running away not from the tigers but from the journalists themselves. It wasn't even as though they stuck to stories about the tigers. Malham was so much in the news that any piece of information would do. Look what had happened to Jenny Wiggins. Jenny had told some nice lady from a tabloid paper about how her mum had run off with her dad's brother a few years ago. Her mum had come back after a few days and Jenny wasn't supposed to know about it.

The next day, Jenny's mum, who ran the local shop

and Post Office, was sorting through the newspapers when she came across this headline: 'MAN-EATING POSTMISTRESS LEAVES FAMILY FOR BROTHER IN TIGER VILLAGE.'

The next day, Jenny disappeared to Leeds.

Steve had a good mind to pull a trick like that himself. He could tell the press how much his dad drank – he knew he drank too much, his mother was always on about it.

'I'm a publican ... I like me drink,' he always protested. Steve could see the headlines now: 'MAN DRINKS LIKE FISH IN VILLAGE OF THE TIGERS ...' That'd show them.

Steve hurried along, past the houses of the straggling little village until he left the people behind. On his own again, the injustice and stupidity of him getting sent away flooded over him again.

It was unfair! There was so much he didn't know!

Steve bit his lip. Maybe he should try and tell someone. After all, Lila was a killer. He loved her, but he was horrified by the thought of what she had been doing. Think – she had almost killed his mum! Those men who had committed the massacre at the Tiger Park deserved everything they got, but sooner or later she would kill someone innocent just because they got in the way. What then?

He could save lives! He could convince her to abandon her revenge before she was caught and killed. He had to see her; it was important; and that chance was being taken away. Lila would seek him out again, he was sure of it. He would be gone. He would have let her down.

Steve followed the beck along the road, past the old bridge where another TV crew was filming – it was one of the more picturesque parts of the village – and down past the last houses straggling along as the village petered out. There was no one in sight but as he passed by an old barn, he heard his mother call him angrily ...

'Steven!'

He scowled and looked around. She was following him now! Scared of him going out alone, he supposed. He waited for her to come running down the road.

'Steven! Steven!' called his mother again.

Steve looked around but ... but ...

He had heard that call before ...

His heart leapt in excitement ... and fear.

'Steven! Steven!'

The call was coming from the rocky hill behind the barn. Steve glanced up and down the road. He was out of sight. He stepped behind a wall and ran round behind the barn.

The girl was not there. But the call came again, this time from higher up. A little beck ran down behind the barn to meet up with the main stream some hundred metres or so further on. The call was coming from the rocky, ferny crevice where the stream tumbled down.

Steve began to scramble over the rocks, up the hill. He had wanted this, he had wanted this so much, but now he was scared silly. The last houses were so close but he was already out of sight of the village, hidden behind a steep bank. He was being shown how to get out of the village without being spotted.

He stopped, panting from his rapid climb. Did he

really want to go on? He had been okay so far, but tigers were never truly safe. He stared up the ravine. There, from behind a high distant boulder, he had the briefest glimpse of a pale, anxious little face peering down at him. He put his hands on the stones and pulled himself higher. He had this last chance. He could not go without meeting her again.

11

Tigers

Once, there were forests on the high tops. Giant cattle, lions, hyenas, rhino all lived here then. During the Ice Age a cap of ice two miles thick grew above the land. When it melted, the bodies of these animals were washed away, and their bones can still be found buried in the cracks and crevices gouged out by the water in the great melt. The forests grew again, the animals came back. This time it was man who wiped them out. When the great beasts were gone he turned his attention to the trees. Over the years, he cut them all down.

Tattered, dying remnants of the old forests still grow along steep gullies and ravines. There the trees still blossom and set seed, but each year the sheep nibble the seedlings and ensure nothing new grows. The trees are all over two hundred years old.

Over these bald hills the pale-skinned girl led Steve. It was as well for them that it was growing dark as there was nowhere to hide. Lila crept in the shadows of the drystone walls that criss-crossed all but the highest and most desolate places. Sometimes she crept along the gullies, taking advantage of their thin covering of ancient trees – hawthorn, cherry, oak, ash, elm, alder, birch – all that was left of the dense ancient woodland.

At one point they heard the clatter of a helicopter, a common sound over this part of the Dales since the terrible events at the Tiger Park. Lila, stuck in the open in the middle of yet another bare field, froze and stared about, trying to work out from which side it would emerge. Steve wondered – how many times a day did this fear of discovery come over her? Finally she dived under the bulging overhang of a tumble-down wall. Steve crept in after her, nervous that the mass of balanced rocks might fall. To Lila, that was preferable to discovery. But not for him.

The helicopter clattered out of sight. The two children peered out from under the wall and continued on their way up the hill.

Girl though she was, she kept the strength of her type and rushed over the stones and rough grass. Steve was hard pressed to follow her. She would pass across the fields so easily she could be a hundred metres or more ahead in seconds and out of sight. Steve thought he had lost her several times. But then she would reappear, suddenly peering curiously over a wall, her head cocked as if to say, 'Why are you so slow?'

Finally, she grew impatient with his slowness. As so often, Lila had a solution. Before Steve's eyes the transformation took place. The girl fell. Her face twisted in pain; she spun round as if she were chasing her tail, flung back her head as the stripes flickered on like fire across her body and her face elongated, opened into the animal muzzle, her jaw swelled as the great killing teeth sprouted. Her body grew and the muscles ran like waves under the rich coat. Steve was alone on the hill with the tigress.

He stood regarding her for a moment, trembling at being so close to such a beast. She approached him, and he spread his arms and held her. The tigress sat for a while with him, accepting his embrace. Then, she turned her muzzle and nudged his legs on top of her. With his arms wrapped round the terrible neck, and his feet hooked under her tail, Lila carried Steve at her own speed for the remaining miles across the Dales to their destination.

Before they covered the last mile the tigress shook herself like a dog ridding itself of water, making Steve fall to the ground. She ran on ahead and Steve had the chance to see the transformation in reverse. She rose up, seeming at first to grow bigger. But it was only because she was rising up on her hind legs. Then she shrank suddenly, the burning stripes paled and faded. Her body turned into the slight form of the girl, her deep coat into the sweatshirt and leggings she had worn before – a perfect imitation of the real thing.

They covered the last mile on foot until they reached a wide sunken area, fringed on three sides by a low cliff, not more than two or three metres high. Lila crept along the cliff edge and down a sudden grassy hollow. She paused, glanced back at Steve and sniffed at the stones around the way in. Then she slid underground. Nervously, Steve followed her.

The light from the opening soon receded. The tunnel was narrow at first but then opened up. Steve, far behind in moments, found himself with a choice of paths to go and paused to listen for the way. It was very still.

'Steven! Steven!' He heard her call softly. He turned

left and followed the sound into complete darkness.

There was something about being alone in the pitch darkness with Lila that Steve found terrible. Fear of the dark, fear of being trapped in this tight narrow passage, fear of the tiger – all combined to terrify him. But he would not let his friend down. He pushed on, his hands and knees on the stony floor of the passage, his heart beating wildly.

The tunnel continued for some distance before Steve without any warning bumped into something warm. He almost shouted in terror, because who knew what was down there? More tigers? Sirrah, the big male? But it was Lila. She gave a little squeak as if she was surprised, too. Her breath was coming in strange little gasps. She, like him, was terrified.

'What is it? What is it, Lila?'

Something warm and wet touched his neck. She was licking him. He said, 'Lila?' again.

'Tok,' she said. It was very clear, a strange sound. Steve had heard it before at the Tiger Park. This was tiger talk, a sound they made to each other when communicating. He reached out to touch her; she was still a girl. She began to scratch at the rocks. Reaching forward with his hands, Steve found that she was pulling away stones and rocks from a heap in front of her. He helped, and together they cleared another opening into the rock face. They worked until it was big enough. Lila crawled in. Steve followed behind.

There was the low rattle of stones, the scuff of her against the rock. She was moving away from him into a cavern. It could have been a small cave or a vast empty space for all he knew. What was in here? Steve began to pant with fear.

'Lila?' His voice sounded high and unnatural.

There was a waiting silence around him. Something – was it her? – approached him. In the darkness, Steve could feel the warmth of a great animal before him. He could have wept from fear.

'Lila?' he begged – because it could be another. But it was Lila. She nudged him lightly with her nose, wanting him to come with her. She moved forward again and Steve, swallowing down his fear, followed after her.

Under his hands he felt the coat of the second tiger. It made him cry out. He heard a low sound from Lila, a sort of exquisite moan of sadness. His hand was touching the leg. How cold and still it was. His hands travelled up along the body ... it seemed enormous in the darkness. It felt like he had been crawling for yards trying to find the head. Then, there it was under his fingers. The stiff neck, the cold open jaws, the clammy flesh around the eyes and nose.

'But he's dead, Lila.'

He heard her lie down. She must have known. Did she think he could bring him back to life, or was it just that she needed someone else to know?

Now Lila began to weep, a long, curious series of moans, sad as ships in the night, like cats wailing at dawn but from a throat as round as a man's chest. Steve leaned forward, found her, and lay with his arms around her and his head against hers, trying to comfort her.

It was so sad. There was no place left for the tigers –

not in the forests and fields of India, not in the snow deserts of Siberia, not here behind high fences in the Dales. Only Lila, with her strange powers, was fit to survive in this world.

When her moaning ceased, Steve began to whisper to her, although he had no idea how much she understood.

'Stay with me,' he told her. 'You could be a girl forever. You could learn to speak, come to school. I bet my mum would look after you, she always wanted a girl. I love you, Lila, I love you. Perhaps you could be a tiger sometimes at night – you could run up here in the Dales.' But even as he spoke, the idea of his mum looking after Lila stuck in his throat. 'They'll get you in the end,' he added sadly. 'They can't let you be. They're all scared and jealous of you. Can't you bear to live as a girl? Can't you?'

Whether the tigress understood him or not he never knew. But Lila had other ideas. She stood up and shook herself free of him, took a couple of steps to the entrance of the cave within a cave. Here she turned and called to him, 'Tok!'

Steve began to crawl after her to the outside.

Lila ran on swiftly ahead and Steve had to crawl on his own, painful on his hands and knees over the stony, muddy ground, seeking for the opening by the wind and fresh air on his face. He didn't see the way out until he was almost upon it. They had been underground for over an hour, and by now it was totally dark outside.

Steve crawled out and stood stiffly upright.

It was a clear night. The clouds had blown away but the warm air had not returned. It was icy cold now, crisp and starry. Already a frost was beginning to form on the grass and the cold sides of the rocks. The land smelled glorious, open and fresh after the underground tomb. Steve gulped it down in lungfuls. Lila was nowhere to be seen.

'Stay with me,' he called. 'Stay here ...'

He heard her snort as if in amusement, saw a great dark shadow move away behind the cliff. Alarmed, Steve scrambled after her, but she was already gone. He looked frantically about, over here, this way, that way ... Had he failed her again?

Had she left him for good this time?

Then he heard a huff ...

There she was! Half hidden in the shadows by a wall.

'Lila!' Steve called, in a fright that she had changed her nature as well as her shape and was now hunting him ... But she had already turned and was running, calling to him to hurry after her. Steve took a few steps forward and ...

His long body tipped and his hands struck the cold turf. His head twisted back and in his throat a cry of amazement choked and rasped. His voice was coming out all wrong. His body was coming out all wrong. He tried to stand up again but fell back onto all fours, unable to balance. He felt his spine shoot down his back in an electric spasm, power spreading along his flanks and through his limbs, up his chest and into the massive muscles of his jaw.

Steve leapt forward as if he could escape this; it was like an explosion. And he was racing along, racing, full of power he'd never had before. The world was full of scent and sound he had never known. He stopped with a snort, amazed at it – scent of sheep, rat, mouse, men, roads a mile away, distant houses. And the smell of his own kind, of Lila. How vivid and how rich the dark night was ...

Lila called him again. With a bound, Steve jumped up the two-metre cliff and was after her. A group of sheep leapt out of a hollow at his feet and silently fled. He almost turned to give chase – but that would come later. Tonight, he was on Lila's trail. Transformed, he was no cub, either. Lila, thinking herself the last of her kind, had made for herself a tiger.

Steve never knew what happened that night. He never understood what it was that Lila wanted and why she had returned to him again and again after he had failed to protect Will and Donna, or why she had turned her strength on him in this way. There were no memories, just feelings. Dreams of play and prey, vivid, unaccountable and full of meaning that ebbed away. There were no witnesses – only the tawny owl who hunted voles and mice in the moon shadows under stone walls and white boulders, who saw two tigers, frost in their shaggy coats, mating that night under Pen-y-Ghent.

12

Mr Lee

It was dawn. Steve found himself lying on the grass curled up against a weathered boulder. Something had just happened ...

He stood up and rubbed his arms. He was chilled. There was frost on his clothes. He wasn't wearing much, just jeans, an anorak he'd pulled on when he first went out – was it already another day? He should have been frozen after a night up here. But instead he felt as though the cold ground had only just begun to make itself felt.

Something made him glance down to his feet. All around the frost had blossomed on the rocks and turned the grass to the colour of pearls, but Steve was standing in a circle of bright green grass far larger than himself, as if he had woken up out of the body of some great beast ten times bigger than his own self.

Before him lay the body of a tiger, stretched out on the short, cropped grass. Steve leaned cautiously forward and found himself sniffing at the air. The great beast was dead. Somehow, the body of Sirrah had been dragged out of the cave. He looked huge, as big as a horse. Already, the sun was beginning to melt the frost in his fur. Small water droplets, like a million jewels, glowed and sparkled on his beautiful thick coat.

And Lila ...? He looked about, suddenly alert ... what on earth *had* happened last night? He spotted her at last in a nook in the ribbed white rocks above him – Lila, the girl, staring out over the frosty hills down to the village below.

Lila knew that her run had come to an end. She had done everything she could to save the members of the colony, and failed. The revenge killings had been madness; she had done herself and her kind no good by it. The remaining Triad members were out of the country and she was not so mad or vengeful as to try and follow them to the ends of the earth. But there was still Lee Yung.

The tigress understood very clearly that while he was alive neither she nor any of her kind would be safe. She did not care to spend her days hiding in the form of a girl. The girl was a camouflage, a trick, not herself. Lila was a tiger. If she could not live as a tiger, then she would rather die.

She had no idea that Will was alive. She had seen him shot and as far as she was concerned, that was an end of it. She regarded herself as the last of her kind, but even that had not been the end for her. When there were no tigers left, she had invented one. There was life growing inside her already from her magical union of the previous night. Yet how could Lila bring that life to birth with Lee Yung in the world?

The Triad leader had left Grassington and had gone down to Malham, right into the heart of her territory. Last night she and Steve had gone down to hunt him. They had, of course, got nowhere near the little guest house where he was staying. The village was crawling with police.

Where did she go from here?

The girl left her vantage point in the rocks and climbed down to Steve and the dead body of her mate. She and Steve, still full of the past night, greeted each other as tigers do, by rubbing their heads against each other. Then she walked over to the dead Sirrah, dragged him up and with a huge effort, hoisted him onto her shoulders.

The strength of the tiger is legendary. Tigers have been known to jump straight up a full five metres with a 250 kilo deer clamped in their mouths, or to drag prey weighing more than themselves halfway up a mountain face just to find a comfortable place to eat it. Even as a tiger, Lila was half the size of Sirrah. When she was a girl he was many times her weight. But she retained her strength. She hefted the huge dead beast across her shoulders and began to walk heavily downhill, towards the village.

'Lila – where are you going?' Steve ran after her. Seeing that she was heading down to the village, he began to chatter excitedly. 'What are you going to do? They'll arrest you. Are you going to stay as a girl? It's easier as a girl than as a tiger ...' he began, about to try and talk her into giving up her true form. But then he stopped short.

Steve was different now. His own chatter sounded foolish to him. He had no memories of the previous night, no knowledge of having been a tiger. But he knew that Lila had made him an unimaginable, unaccountable gift, and that he would never be the same again. He had grown up overnight in a way no one had ever done before. She had left inside him forever a streak of the tiger in his soul. He had no idea what she was about to do, but he sensed instinctively that it was a matter of life and death for her, and possibly for him, too. And not human life, either, but the life of a wild animal which is won or lost, with intensity or carelessness, in the blink of an eye.

Keeping his silence he followed her down.

* * *

The big news that night, of course, had been the disappearance of the boy, Steven Hattersly. It had wiped the item about Lee Yung buying the Tiger Park with all its debts, off the front pages. Everyone had known how wild Steve was about the tigers, how upset he had been by their disappearance. Had he become Lila's latest victim? When he failed to return home the previous evening the police had organised a huge manhunt. They had teams of men with dogs, shouting in the cold, soft light of the northern evening, hoping he was still alive and might call back. But there was no answer. Darkness came and the search was abandoned for the night.

In the meantime all anyone could do was hope that he had simply hidden in order to avoid having to leave Malham while all the excitement was still going on, or that he had wandered onto the hills and got lost. By all accounts he wasn't wearing much. Really, the cold was a greater killer than the tigress. It was an easy matter to freeze to death on these hills.

With the return of light a large body of policemen and volunteers were gathering just outside Malham, ready to resume the search. The village was in a trauma. It was what everyone had feared – that the tragedy of the Tiger Park had at last reached into their own community.

Few other people were about. A number of TV journalists getting some footage for the morning news hung about round the police. A milkman, a few farmers about their business in the village. The police, gathered around their vehicles and checking their plans, were just about ready to set off to various locations on the hills when a beat-up old Land-Rover came revving down the road towards them. An old Yorkshire farmer leaned out and regarded them gravely.

'Bloody police, in wrong place at wrong time agin.' He nodded his head backwards into the village. 'Our Steven's down thata way. And he's only got bloody tiger with him!' There was a pause while the police worked out whether the old man was serious or not. Then, a sudden rustle of alarm. The police grabbed their guns, the TV crews their cameras and sound equipment, and the whole mass of them started running heavily back towards the village.

'It's all right, you won't need guns, it's a dead 'en!'

The farmer watched in amusement as the police went hurtling helter-skelter down the road, boots clattering on the tarmac.

'Show-off coppers. Boggers'd shoot sheep if they thowt it'd impress Kate Adie,' muttered the old man to his dog. Then he turned the vehicle round and followed, at a sensible distance, to watch. He was curious to see how they'd react when they saw that there was also a slightly-built girl carrying the huge dead tiger over her back.

When they saw it, the police ground to a halt. It was ... not possible. Even for a full-grown man ...

The girl was so tiny! The tiger hung down on either side like a dragon. For a full ten seconds the stunned policemen and journalists stared as the tiny figure, staggering only slightly under the huge weight, pressed on down the village street and flung the great beast down on the ground before a guest house on the edge of the village. Then there was a sudden scrabble as the TV crews got their cameras up and started shooting.

The police got their wits back. This was obviously the girl they had been asking after, whose footprints had been found in blood in the tiger compound over a week ago now. She – and the boy – would have to be taken in for questioning. A senior officer, once he was quite sure by the smell that the big tiger was truly dead, stepped forward to take her arm.

Then the impossible happened.

It happened in full view – before the TV cameras, before the policemen, before the entire village. The girl fell to her knees and out of her, like a fantastic plant, a new shape began to grow. It blossomed before their eyes, pale orange striped, fantastic, dangerous. There, where the girl had stood, stood the tiger. She crouched, a miracle on the damp road and stared fixedly at a window on the first floor of the guest house.

The policeman fell back with a cry of shock. Others screamed and yelled and began to run. Steve understood at once what was required of him. He moved with the speed of a cat himself and flung himself at Lila before

143

the armed men could even lift their weapons.

'Don't shoot! Don't shoot! You'll hit me!' he screamed. His eyes were tightly closed in fear of the hail of bullets he was sure were about to come his way. He pressed himself hard along the full length of her body.

The hubbub rose up, a welter of confused voices and scared men. But it worked – for the moment. No one dared shoot for fear of hitting the boy.

Out of the chaos of voices came one more.

'Lee Yung! Lee Yung!' cried a voice. Everyone went still and stared incredulously. It was the voice of the tiger.

Lila settled herself like a spring on her haunches, her eyes still fixed on that window.

'Lee Yung! Lee Yung!' she called. 'Lee Yung. I ... have ... come.'

Mr Lee was still in his bed when he heard the voice from outside. He had been ready to expect anything, but now he was scared. He flung back the covers. Outside the window were voices, a mumble of fear.

'Please walk slowly away from the tiger,' he heard someone saying in a shaky voice. 'Walk away slowly. She is very dangerous.'

The door opened and a number of his personal bodyguards ran in.

'She has come, Mr Lee, the tiger. She outside. She is ... calling you.'

Lee Yung knew very well that if he saw the tiger she would try to take him with her eye just as she had done before, outside the hotel in Grassington. But that was no threat for him. She was down there, he was up here, and, more to the point, he was surrounded by both the police and his own men, all armed.

He swung his legs out of bed and got shakily to his feet. In his pyjamas, he looked slighter than ever. The bony ridge under his neck showed how the illness had stripped his body of flesh. But his will to live was as fierce as ever.

'Do not shoot unless she goes for me,' he told his men. 'If she dies now I might find it hard to get the body. Leave it to the Park Rangers with their anaesthetic darts. We can take her later, at our leisure. Remember – I own this tiger.'

He watched closely to see that they understood. Many of the men found it difficult to follow instructions when it came to dealing with a creature that had more than one shape. They were, quite rightly, superstitious about such beasts. But these were excellent men, soldiers in suits, hand-picked for the job. He could rely on them to follow orders.

Lee Yung pulled on a dressing-gown and opened the curtains. For a second he looked down through the glass and then, at a word from him, one of the men opened the window.

Lila was sitting on the ground outside the building. At first sight the village streets were empty but a second glance showed up the police, hiding behind every corner, peering from every door and every window. Around the neck of the tiger, clinging as if he were a second skin, was a boy.

Lee Yung frowned. He should have been told. He turned to his men. 'Remember – if she goes for me you are to kill her – even if it means hitting the boy.'

'Understood.' A crop of guns appeared around him as they took aim.

'If I try to reach her you are to stop me. Understood?'

'Yes, sir!'

So – she had found a protector. She was even cleverer than he had thought.

Lee Yung looked down to the tigress. 'Lila,' he called softly. He smiled at her. He had no idea that she had transformed herself in full view of the eyes of the world. He believed he was in possession of her secret. Maybe the boy knew. But no one else would ever dream ...

'Lila,' he called again. He would have liked her to speak back.

Below on the ground Lila's jaw worked – as if she could utter everything she knew. Then, her body stiffened, and her eye bored into Mr Lee.

He felt it – his hands dropped down, his head wagged loosely on his neck and drooped. He felt it – but he did not fear it. He had explained to his men that this might happen. He could hear them muttering. They did not like it but they had their orders. Indeed, Lee Yung was so sure of himself that he felt pleasure. He was safe. It was almost a pleasure to feel her power because soon that power would be his. He would drink her blood, eat her heart – the heart of the Spirit Tiger. He would be made well. He would become a more powerful man than ever.

He tried to lift his head, to test her. They both knew

she was stronger, but that he would win. He was able to lift his head. Triumphantly he looked right into her eyes. He could see the glowing amber, the power.

Lila reached right inside ...

In that moment Lee Yung knew he had made a dreadful mistake. He tried to open his mouth, make his tongue work to tell his men to pull him away but his mouth was frozen. He choked, gasped and ...

Steve heard the sudden gagging noise above him from the window. He looked up just in time to see Lee Yung tip suddenly forward and tumble half out of the window. His men lunged for him. One of them managed to seize him by the hand. The little body hung for a moment out of the window like a doll, dangling from one arm. He seemed to be held together only by his skin. Then the big men leaned down out of the window and dragged him back up into the room. Steve caught a brief glimpse of a gun waving furiously at him and Lila, but the thugs were confused with their master so strangely defeated, and were too scared to hit a child. The window slammed suddenly shut.

Lee Yung had underestimated Lila for the last time. The tigress had reached right inside him with her gaze ... and stopped his heart.

Steve felt the tiger sigh. He leaned heavily against her, loving her. He felt suddenly exhausted. The tigress had used up every scrap of him. 'It's safe now – please stop. Please stop,' be begged. He loved her, be she girl or beast, but she was too much. 'Be a girl again,' he begged.

Lila looked sideways at him, and snarled.

'Lila?' In surprise, Steve took a couple of steps back. Lila snarled again – there was no mistaking it – the head up, the ears laid back. Steve took two steps back.

'Get back, boy ... get back ...'

Steve looked up to see the tall figure of Mike Craven, standing half hidden behind a corner with his dart rifle. The streets were clear by now, but all around out of windows and doorways, the armed policemen peered.

'Get back so I can get a shot at her with the darts before the police open fire. Get back, for God's sake – quick!' Steve gave Lila one last look of love and fear. Then he began to back off.

At her place under the open window, Lila watched out of the corner of her eye as the boy ran out of sight behind a corner. It was over at last. Now she turned her gaze inwards and with her last act of power, burnt out the heart of magic within her. There would be no more girl, no more plans or acts of vengeance, no more magic. She destroyed her soul as a sacrifice. She only wanted now to share in the fate of her species.

Feeling suddenly exposed, aware as if for the first time of the hordes of humans hidden all around her, the tigress sprang to her feet and took a few rapid steps away from the buildings. At the same moment something struck her in the shoulder. She lashed out at nothing. The drug began to take effect at once. She nipped with her teeth at the dart even as her hind legs gave way, then her forelegs.

She sank onto her side. Her lips curled back in a half snarl and as the darkness closed in, she laid her head down with a vague notion of having to wait to see what her captors would do with her.